A KEY
TO DEATH

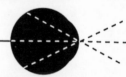

A KEY
TO DEATH

A Mr. and Mrs. North Mystery

Frances and Richard
Lockridge

Thorndike Press • Thorndike, Maine

L.P.
MYST
L.

Library of Congress Cataloging in Publication Data:

Lockridge, Frances Louise Davis.
   A key to death : a Mr. and Mrs. North mystery /
by Frances and Richard Lockridge.
      p.   cm.
   ISBN 1-56054-183-0 (alk. paper : lg. print)
   1. Large type books. I. Lockridge, Richard, 1898-
II. Title.
[PS3523.O243K4   1991]   91-3570
813'.54—dc20   CIP

Thorndike Press Large Print edition published in 1991
by arrangement with HarperCollins Publishers.

Large Print edition available in the British Commonwealth by arrangement with Curtis Brown, Ltd.

Cover design by James B. Murray.

The tree indicium is a trademark of Thorndike Press.

This book is printed on acid-free, high opacity paper.∞

A KEY
TO DEATH

I

Forbes Ingraham hung his topcoat in the closet and brushed dampness from thick, graying hair. He crossed the office and sat in the leather chair behind the shining large desk with its fresh blotter, its two well-dusted telephones. He sat with his back to windows against which February rain lashed, driven by a gusty wind. But for all the anger of the wind, the rain was no more than the softest rustling in the big room, in which all sounds were muted.

Ingraham fitted a cigarette into his holder, lighted it and leaned back in the chair and waited for the day to begin. A telephone rang and he picked it up, without surprise. In this, poor Mary's timing was so precise — so many seconds for him to walk from the reception room and through the library; so many more to hang up a coat in the office closet, to cross the room to his desk, then to light a cigarette. She might have used a stopwatch, but the only

7

clock she used ticked in her gentle, but in too many respects lamentably fuzzy, mind. She clung to this precision; in this she did not fail. Ingraham shook his head, the smile on his flexible lips diminishing. Last week, he had waited patiently at the Pierre to lunch with a man who waited, less patiently, at the Roosevelt, and that, also, was Mary's doing.

Having rung once, and rung in a whisper, the telephone had not repeated itself. Ingraham said "Yes?" into it, in a soft voice.

"Good morning, Mr. Ingraham," Mrs. Mary Burton said from the outer office, and he said, in the same soft, unhurrying voice, "Good morning, Mary. Was it wet on Staten Island, too?"

"Oh yes," Mary said. "And the ferry — goodness!"

It was wet on Staten Island; it was snowy, or windy, or hot — but there was almost always a nice breeze there — or not anything in particular. Five mornings of each week, save for a month in summer, two weeks in winter, Forbes Ingraham was informed of these meteorological triumphs or mishaps of the Borough of Richmond, about which he could hardly have cared less.

"What have we today, Mary?" Forbes Ingraham said, in the same gentle voice and, while he listened, checked against his own memory; against, also, notations on the top sheet of the yellow pad in front of him.

"Mr. Halpern," he repeated. "Yes, I know he is. Not here yet?"

Mr. Halpern, it appeared, was not.

Mr. Cuyler would like to see him when he had a moment free, and to this Ingraham said "Yes," in the same tone. Mr. Webb had some things he wanted to go over, when it could be worked in. A Mr. Michael Fergus — was that right? — was down for eleven-thirty, but if Mr. Halpern was really late —

"Yes, Mary."

At noon, the people from NBC, and Mr. Phelps, and his client, Miss Waterhouse — but of course, Mr. Ingraham remembered about that.

"Miss Waterhouse, Mary?"

"That's what — oh, dear. Miss Masterson, isn't it?"

"I believe so, Mary."

At one-fifteen, if he could make it, Mr. Fleming at the Pierre. "It's really the Pierre this time, Mr. Ingraham. I've double checked and — I'm so *wretched* about that, Mr. Ingraham."

"Yes, Mary."

"And Mr. and Mrs. North at three and then at three-thirty, Mrs. Schaeffer. There doesn't seem to be anything after that."

"No, Mary," Forbes Ingraham said, and there was a line vertical in his broad forehead. "I don't recall anything after Mrs. Schaeffer."

"Mr. Brown's secretary called twice and will you —"

"No, Mary. It's their hurry, not ours. Ask Mrs. Lynch to bring the mail in."

"Oh — I'm afraid she's in Mr. Webb's office. Shall I send Phyllis?"

"No, Mary. I'd rather you brought it yourself, then. And tell Mr. Cuyler —"

"Mr. Halpern just came in."

"Mr. Halpern, then. But bring the mail first. And see if you can get Armstrong in Philadelphia, and if you do put him through. But not anyone else, Mary."

The last injunction was habitual; it was also hopeless. If Mary Burton remembered, which she did infrequently, she was susceptible to almost any plea of urgency. Poor Mary.

The mail came; after the mail, which turned out to be of the kind which can wait, Mr. Halpern.

Mr. Halpern was a big man, in a blue suit not quite big enough. He looked as if he had worked much out of doors; perhaps, although he was in his sixties, still did. His jaw was noticeably long. He had a heavy voice, which rasped a little. He had a good deal to say, and Forbes Ingraham leaned back in the leather chair, and listened. Ingraham's rather broad, very clever face, was almost expressionless. He smoked, the long holder clenched in regular, white teeth. Now and then he nodded his head. At one remark in Halpern's rasping voice, Ingraham smiled faintly, and shook his head. He took the holder from between his teeth and said, "I don't think it'll come to that, Mr. Halpern."

"You don't know this crowd," Halpern said. "They're tough bastards. If they don't pin this on me —"

"Oh yes," Ingraham said. "I do understand. That's why we're taking the case. You realize it's out of our line."

"Yeah. I know that," Halpern said. "Appreciate it. All the boys appreciate it. So — here's the stuff you wanted."

Ingraham took the stuff, which occupied a large envelope. He said he would tell Mr. Halpern what he thought tomorrow. He leaned forward, then, and turned back the top sheet on the yellow pad. He made several notes on the pad, said, in the soft voice which nevertheless had unusual carrying power, "Same time all right?" and, being told it was, got up and walked with the taller man out of the office, and through the library to the reception room. The reception room was empty, after Mr. Halpern left it.

11

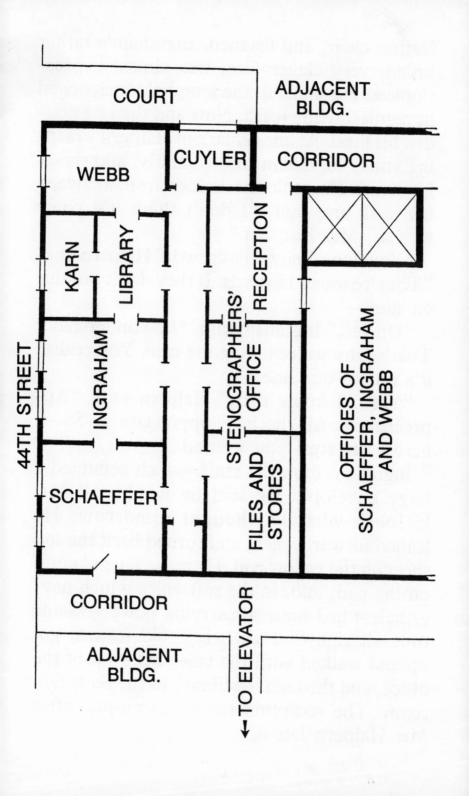

"Oh, Mr. Ingraham," Mary Burton said, and her head appeared at the information window in one wall of the reception room. She looked a little, framed so, like another of the prints of bewigged English judges which hung numerously on the walls. Ingraham supposed that this was somehow connected with the regularity in the curls of Mary Burton's white hair. It was true, of course, that she had, also, a rather long face. There was still a kind of eagerness in it. Poor Mary.

"Mr. Armstrong won't be in until after lunch," Mary said. Her face was worried. "I told them it was important, but —" She waited exculpation for failure.

"Not your fault, Mary," Forbes Ingraham told her, and went back into the inner corridor. He went down it, away from his office, to a door at the end of the corridor, and opened it.

"I keep telling you —" a tall man who stood behind a desk was saying — saying with emphasis, with feeling — to a slender, pretty girl with a shining cap of silvery blond hair — "that whatever he —" The man stopped speaking abruptly. He turned from the girl toward Forbes Ingraham, and ran his right hand through black hair, pushing it back. His eyes were black in a white face. "Oh!" the girl said, and said involuntarily.

13

"Morning, Frank," Ingraham said, in the soft voice which yet seemed to have more weight in the little room than the other man's had had, for all its emphasis. Ingraham nodded to the girl, and said, "Phyllis."

She looked quickly from one man to the other. She flushed.

"I'm —" she said, but shook her head.

"That's all, then, Miss Moore," the black-haired man said, and she said, "Yes, Mr. Cuyler," and Ingraham opened the door for her. He closed it after her.

"Mary says you've something to take up with me, Frank," Forbes Ingraham said. "If it won't take too long —"

It did not take long. Ingraham left the smaller office of Francis Cuyler, an associate of the firm of Schaeffer, Ingraham and Webb, at about eleven thirty-five and met Dorothy Lynch just outside the door. She was going, carrying her notebook, from the office of Reginald Webb back to the office, with its window on the reception room, she shared with Mary Burton and Phyllis Moore, and the office boy, Eddie Smythe, who was seventeen and much bothered about his complexion.

Mr. Michael Fergus had been prompt. He was in the reception room when, returning from Francis Cuyler's office, Ingraham reached it. Mr. Fergus was short, and broad, and had mustaches, which were formidable, and a beard. He sat, his knees spread and his hands on knees, in the precise middle of a leather sofa, and his attitude was that of a man who rejects comfort and is, indeed, about to spring. Years ago men of his appearance had been caricatured as anarchists; now they were considered prototypes of all Russians. Mr. Fergus had been born in Ohio; he wrote magazine serials in which young men of mild appearance turned intrepid adventurers, so disconcerting villainy and winning the affections of young women of pleasing anatomical structure. Despite his appearance, Mr. Fergus was devoutly Republican.

"Good morning, Mike," Forbes Ingraham said, in his gentle voice. Mr. Fergus surged forward. He clasped Ingraham's hand; he appeared to shake his beard at Ingraham. He was ushered into the big office, and there sat on another leather sofa, his position as before. Forbes Ingraham inserted a fresh cigarette in his holder and lighted it. He lifted one of the telephones and said, "Will you send the Fergus contracts in, please," and put it down again.

"I'm not sure we can give them what they want, Mike," he said, speaking slowly. "Unless we can get them to hold up until —"

Dorothy Lynch brought the contracts. She was trim; in all respects, from prettily shod feet to carefully ordered brown hair, she was of precision design. She smiled at Michael Fergus, who waved his beard at her pleasantly; she put a sheaf of papers neatly in front of Forbes Ingraham, and was thanked, and went. "A glacial type," Michael Fergus said, after the door closed on her. To this, Ingraham said only, and with impartiality, "Hm-m." He leafed the contracts. "Here," he said. "This is what can give us trouble." He pointed. "We can't be sure how the courts would construe, if it came to that. On the other hand —"

Michael Fergus emerged from the big office a little before twelve, and his beard appeared to droop a little; it was even possible that he muttered into it. Ingraham watched him go, smiling faintly. He used the telephone, being connected with Reginald Webb.

"Morning, Reg," Ingraham said. "Mary says you seek conference. I've got five minutes or so if —"

"It's nothing important," Webb said. "Thought you might like to look over the draft on the Avery answer. But since you were tied up —"

"You know more about it than I do," Ingraham told him. "You want to sit in on a lunch with Fleming?"

"Not," Webb said, with emphasis, "if I can help it, Forbes."

16

Forbes Ingraham made a small sound of amusement.

"By the way," Webb said, "is Nan coming in today?"

"Yes. This afternoon."

Ingraham waited briefly for comment. He received none.

"I've got a call in for Armstrong," he said then. "I'll be tied up with this NBC crowd and Miss Masterson's troubles for an hour or so. Incidentally, Mary's decided it's 'Waterhouse.' You know, Reg, we'll —" The other telephone rang, interrupting him. "Anyway," he finished, "you want to talk to Armstrong if it comes through?"

He waited only for, "Sure, I'll talk to him," and turned to the other telephone. He learned that the NBC people and Miss Waterson and her agent waited. He sighed, and asked that they be sent in.

It was almost one-thirty when he got to the Pierre Grill, and it was a little after three when he got back to the offices of Schaeffer, Ingraham and Webb in a building of mature dignity in West Forty-fourth Street. Mr. and Mrs. Gerald North awaited him.

"So," Forbes Ingraham said, "you made it, finally." He pointed at them with his cigarette holder.

"Because we're driving, instead of by train,"

Pam North said. "And Cousin Wilmer, of course."

Ingraham nodded gravely, or almost gravely. He had known Pamela for several years; had no doubt that all, in time, would be clarified.

"Wilmer," Pam said, "is ailurophobe, but even without that we've decided that blood isn't thicker than water — not Cousin Wilmer's blood, anyway."

It was Jerry, standing, who ran a hand through his hair.

"It really does make sense," he said. He considered. "It did, anyway," he added. "Before —" He looked at his wife.

"Yes," Ingraham said. "Well, come on —"

"Oh, Mr. Ingraham," Mary Burton said, her long face, her waved white hair, appearing in the information window. "Now they say Mr. Armstrong's gone for the day, but if I tried his club —"

"Yes, Mary," Ingraham said. "Do that, will you? And not put anything through, except him if you get him, for the next half hour?"

"Of course," Mary Burton said. "I do hope it was the Pierre. After you'd gone I got to worrying whether —"

"Yes, Mary," Ingraham said, and took the Norths into his office. It was hot there. Ingraham opened one of the windows a few inches. Damp coolness came in, and street noises. He sat the Norths side by side on a leather sofa. He offered cigarettes, fitted one into his own holder. He said that he was glad that they had finally got around to it. He added that no lawyer likes to have his clients die intestate.

"As things are at the moment," Gerald North said, somewhat morosely, "it wouldn't make a great deal of difference. But Pam feels we ought to try to provide for the cats. And that the stretch between Jacksonville and Miami is —" He shrugged. "So," he said.

"Well," Pam said, "we couldn't get anything except two roomettes, not even in the same end of the car. This way, if we run into a truck or something, we'll be together, anyway. Which is the point, of course." She looked at Forbes Ingraham. "About our making our wills," she said, explaining all. "Before we go to Florida."

Forbes Ingraham nodded, still with gravity.

"Isn't it true," Pam said, "that they assume the woman died first? Being the weaker vessel? In spite of the fact that women live longer than men? Generally speaking, of course?"

There was no rule about it, Ingraham said

— at least no rule which was universal. Courts had so held. Courts had held almost everything one could imagine.

"Then," Pam said, "when we hit this truck, Jerry inherits from me but Wilmer inherits from Jerry, being his only relative. And there's nothing left for the cats. It would be like Wilmer to have them killed, only he'd say put to sleep, probably. He says things like that. But the aunts, on the other hand, would be good to the cats." She paused. "Even Martini," she said, "if she'd let them."

"I take it," Forbes Ingraham said, and pulled toward him the yellow pad. Half a dozen sheets were filled with his neat, small writing, and turned back. He wrote "Norths" at the top of a fresh sheet. "I take it," he said, "that you don't want to leave money to the cats, as such? Or in trust for them?"

"Heavens no!" Pam said. "It always sounds so silly in the papers. 'Mr. and Mrs. Gerald North, under the terms of wills filed for probate today, left their estate, estimated at' — hm-m. Anyway, to three cats named Martini and Gin and Sherry. It would be embarrassing."

Not, Jerry pointed out, under the circumstances she had, perhaps a little morbidly, assumed — not to them.

"What you want," Ingraham said, "is everything to each other, if surviving; then the aunts — you'll have to give me their names, Pam — then — then what?"

"The Authors League Fund," Jerry said, and looked enquiringly at his wife.

"I'd as soon authors as anybody," Pam said. "The poor things."

She gave the names of the aunts; they agreed on executors; it was all simple enough, and painless enough. With notes completed, Ingraham leaned back. He would draw the wills up, have them typed. The next day they would —

A telephone rang. Ingraham spoke into it softly, briefly. He said, "I'll call you back." He hung up, took the other telephone from its cradle and said into it, "Please, Mary. I told you —"

"Come in and sign," he said. "With witnesses, in your presence and in the presence of each other. About this time all right?"

The morning would be better, Jerry said. They compromised on noon.

"While you're here," Ingraham said, then, and talked briefly, in his soft voice, of a plagiarism suit threatened against North Books, Inc., for which Schaeffer, Ingraham and Webb were counsel. He did not, Ingraham said, regard the suit as especially threatening.

"Sam probably told you that," he said. "We went over it together before I went abroad. Of course, we'll watch it."

He had leaned forward as he spoke; now he leaned back again. He lighted a fresh cigarette. He looked across the room, at the opposite wall, and there was a line vertical in his broad forehead.

"Sam Schaeffer had a damn good mind," he said, to the distant wall.

Jerry North said, after a brief pause, that he had been sorry to hear. Forbes Ingraham looked at him, at Pam. He nodded.

"One of those senseless accidents," he said. "Happen all the time, but — hard to accept, all the same."

He paused. "Still expect him to open that door" — he gestured toward a door in a side wall of the big office — "and walk in — and you always thought of Heywood Broun and the 'unmade bed' — and say, 'Ingraham, I'd like you to look at this.' Great man for last names, Sam was. And almost everybody called him Sam, and he liked it.

"Senseless damn thing," Forbes Ingraham said again. "Keep wanting things to make sense. You'd think I'd learn, wouldn't you?"

"Everybody does," Pam said. "And things don't."

"Well," Forbes said, "we've still got to try

to make them, I suppose."

In the street below, a truck backfired with violence, and somebody leaned on a car's horn. Ingraham reached back and closed the window. They would never imagine, he said, that the office was sound-proofed. With the result that people could shoot off firecrackers in the hall outside, or yell their heads off for help, and he'd never hear them. But the traffic four floors below might as well be in the room. If —

The telephone rang, softly. Ingraham answered it in his soft voice. He said "Yes," and again said "Yes." He said, "In about five minutes," and put the telephone gently back in its cradle. The Norths were standing by then, and Ingraham stood too, and came from behind his desk. But his movements were unhurried. He helped Pamela with her coat; he said, looking out a window, that he envied them their trip south. He walked with them to the door, and through the library to the reception room.

A slender woman in her thirties sat on the leather sofa, in the company of a mink coat. She smiled up at Forbes Ingraham when he appeared behind the Norths, and crushed out a cigarette in an ashtray. She gathered the mink toward her and Ingraham said, "Hello, Nan. With you in a minute," and crossed the

23

reception room with the Norths to the door. He said, "About noon, then," and opened the door for them and saw them through it. Outside, Pam said, "Such a nice man" and, "that mink must have cost thousands." Gerald North, no man to arouse sleeping minks, rang for the elevator.

The rain had stopped; the wind blew gustily through Forty-fourth Street, but now from the northwest. It bustled the Norths toward the east; when a cab stopped for them, it bounced them into the cab and, down the avenue, toward home, the cab seemed to scud with the wind. They were safe inside the apartment, and had greeted the cats — Pam assured the cats that it was being arranged for them to be taken care of if "anything happens" — before Pam reminded Jerry that they were not destined to remain there.

"Margaret's cocktail party," she said and then, "Don't tell me you've forgotten," just as Jerry was about to. Jerry said, "Oh, *no*, Pam," and was told that they had promised. "And," Pam said, "it isn't raining any more," to clinch matters.

"Not one of *those*," Jerry said, seeming to beseech higher power than Pam. "Why? What's she celebrating?"

"I suppose," Pam said, "the arrival of five-thirty. Or six, really. You'll like it, once you're there."

He liked Margaret, Jerry said. They would not see Margaret, except for an instant on arrival, perhaps another on departure. But these parties of hers —

"They," Jerry said firmly, "constitute unlawful assembly. Or loitering with intent. Why can't we —"

"We promised," Pam said. "Also, it may be fun — sometimes they are. Everybody'll be there."

"God knows," Jerry said, morosely.

"Well," Pam told him, "that's who she knows — everybody." She considered this. "Everybody we know, anyway," she said, compromising.

"That man she has," Jerry said, "makes martinis in advance. Pours them out of a bottle. Listen — once I got one with an olive *and* lemon peel."

If this would not dissuade Pam from party going, nothing would. It did not . . .

Margaret lived on Park Avenue, in an inflated apartment. She had been, for twenty years, the dutiful wife of an older man who shared — who exaggerated — Jerry North's distaste for social gatherings. He referred to them as brawls, and considered them blessed neither to give nor to receive. He had died

— rather appropriately, alone in a hotel room while on a business trip — and his wife, after a decent interval of regret, had begun to make up for lost parties. She was pretty and blond — rather like a fluffy kitten — and in her middle forties. When the Norths arrived a little after six, she greeted them as *"darlings!"* and assured them that they would know everybody and gently brushed them into a tremendous room which reminded Jerry of Grand Central at five-ten, except that nobody was running.

They did not know everybody. At first, indeed, it appeared that they did not know anybody. Bereft of hostess — who could be expected to return, but was now saying *"darlings!"* to an arriving group of four — the Norths stood, wearing party smiles which fitted a little tightly, and watched strangers drink. In the distance, to be glimpsed as if in a forest, a man in a white jacket moved slowly, carrying a tray. He did not seem to approach.

"What it is," Jerry said, after several minutes — "what it is, we're in a dead spot. Come on."

They went, slowly, smiling the smiles of those who are co-guests without being acquaintances, feeling like new members of a country club, in the direction taken by the man in the white coat. Progress was tentative, of necessity somewhat apologetic, wary of jostling. Eventually, seeming to have got no place in particular, it stopped.

"We seem to be hemmed in," Pam said. "We —"

"The Norths," a softly pleasant voice said behind Jerry. "Still alive, I see."

"Well," Pam said. "Such a small world."

"It is," Forbes Ingraham said, "part of the service of the firm. Can't have you dying before you sign, you know." He looked at their empty hands. "Of thirst, apparently," he added. "He went thataway." He indicated, with a movement of his handsome head. "He —"

"*Darlings!*" Margaret said, emerging in a small clearing nearby. "You haven't anything to *drink!*"

"No," Jerry said.

"We'll have to do —" Margaret said, but then the clearing closed around her and she vanished.

"I can't," Pam North said, "remember ever seeing so many tall people."

"These are the Norths," Forbes Ingraham said, and pulled a slender woman from between two masculine backs. The woman had warmly brown hair and through it a streak intensely white. Her smooth skin was deeply tanned. She said, "I know they are."

"Mrs. James," Forbes said. "Phoebe James."

"At," Phoebe James said, "one of those terrible do's in Pittsburgh, wasn't it? I mean, very nice do's, actually. Book and author."

"When you were an author and we were a book," Pam said.

Phoebe James grinned at her. The grin was widely white in her tanned face.

"Darlings!" Margaret said, emerging from a new direction. "I've got somebody coming." She beamed at the Norths, at Forbes Ingraham and Phoebe James. "So nice you've all —" she said, but was submerged again.

But then a man in a white jacket broke through, and offered drinks. The Norths took martinis — which this time contained no added oddities. Forbes Ingraham exchanged an empty highball glass for one not empty; Phoebe James, whose last historical novel had perched in eminence, and for months, near the top of the list, shook her white-streaked head.

Jerry raised his glass, thankfully, and his elbow was bumped from behind by someone who was *"Terribly* sorry," and with that was gone. The tipped glass spilled half its contents down Jerry North's sleeve. It was, under the circumstances, no consolation at all to discover that, this time, the drinks had been made cold enough.

"Jerry!" Pam said. "You shouldn't talk that way."

Jerry North drank what remained in his glass. He drank it too quickly. He choked.

II

"Then," Pamela North said. "One thing led to another. But — do you want all this?"

She looked down at her hands. They were shaking a little. She clasped them together to stop the shaking. Jerry put a hand briefly on her shoulder, and said nothing. She turned, and managed to smile, and to nod her head in a way which meant that she would be all right, was all right.

"I don't know, Pam," Bill Weigand said. "I don't know what I want."

"It — it happened today."

"Right," Bill said. "It happened today. But — things like this don't happen only at one time, at one minute of one day, between ten minutes of eleven and ten after. They happen yesterday — and a week ago yesterday, and a month before that."

They sat in a small office, with one large window on a court. The wind, more gusty even than it had been the night before, swept down into the court, found itself trapped there, swirled angrily in an attempt to escape. The wide window rattled in the fury of the trapped wind.

"Well," Pam said, "the four of us — Jerry and me, Forbes and Mrs. James — we —"

They had begun to edge their way out of the center of the crowded party, seeking some zone of quiet, some more placid backwater. They had made slow going of it, but it had been managed. They had met, along the tortuous way, people they knew, people to be greeted across intervening strangers, waved at from a distance.

"Mr. Ingraham too?"

Ingraham too; Phoebe James more than any of them, which was to be expected. She was a person it was gratifying to know, by whom to be recognized. But the four of them had more or less stayed together, and in the end had found haven.

"At least," Pam said, "we got into a corner, sort of. And a man did come with drinks again, and another man with canapés. I had a cigarette and a glass and then, because he poked them at me, a canapé, all at once, and —"

"You met Mr. Ingraham's partner there? Reginald Webb? And Mrs. Schaeffer? You were with them when Mr. Ingraham got a telephone call?"

"Was there something special about the telephone call?"

"I don't know," Bill said. "Webb seems to think there was. He said that Ingraham appeared to be startled. Did you think that?"

"Not then so much as earlier," Pam said. "At least — didn't you think so, Jerry?"

"I don't know," Jerry North said. "I wasn't thinking about much of anything, except how to get the hell out of there. That is, I didn't think so then. When Pam and I were talking later, it did come back that Forbes's attitude had changed before the telephone call. But — it's not very tangible, Bill."

Forbes Ingraham had been as soft-spoken, as unaggressively assured as always, when the four of them first stood in the corner of the room, the party swirling before them. He had held a long cigarette holder in white teeth and, with the rest, talked easily. They had talked primarily of books, as became a famous author, a publisher and an attorney who specialized in the affairs of authors fortunate enough to have affairs, and of publishers successful enough to afford him.

"Mrs. James is one of his clients," Pam said. "Only — it occurred to me, more than that. From something in their attitudes toward each other. Was I right?"

"I don't know yet," Bill said. "It's quite

possible, of course. She's divorced. Ingraham never seems to have married. Go on, Pam."

But, saying something about the vagaries of libel laws, telling a story about them, Ingraham had stopped in the middle of a sentence, and looked off into the crowd. "As if," Pam said now, "he saw something that worried him." But the interruption had lasted only seconds; he had taken up the story again. It was after that that Webb and Mrs. Schaeffer had joined them, and been introduced.

"That is," Jerry said, "Mrs. Schaeffer was. We'd met Webb before, of course — or I had. You had too, hadn't you Pam?"

"Once or twice," Pam said. "At first, last night, he was just a quite tall man with a brush hair cut. Very well dressed. But with hair getting a little thin at the top. All the other hairs very — aggressive. To make up for the deserters. We'd seen Mrs. Schaeffer too, of course. But not to speak to."

The Mrs. Schaeffer of the cocktail party had been the beautifully groomed, slender woman who sat with mink on the sofa in the reception room of Schaeffer, Ingraham and Webb — the widow of Samuel Schaeffer.

"Who," Pam said, "died accidentally a while back. Forbes — Forbes was telling us."

"Webb and Mrs. Schaeffer were together? I mean — obviously they were then. Did you

33

have —" Bill Weigand paused. He looked at Pam, as if in doubt about a word. "Any intuition about them? As you had about Ingraham and Mrs. James?"

"If there's one word I hate," Pam North said. "People just use their minds and people talk about — *intuition.*"

Bill Weigand waited.

"No," Pam said. "I didn't notice anything especially. What do *they* say? And what would it have to do with — with this, anyway?"

"They haven't been asked," Bill said. "I don't know that it has anything. There were six in a group, then, when Mr. Ingraham got this telephone call?"

It had not been, exactly, a telephone call. A man — one of the men in white coats — had come through the party to Forbes Ingraham and spoken to him and, after listening, Ingraham had said, "The hell he does."

"And seemed annoyed?"

For a moment, possibly. Phoebe James — "she has the loveliest voice, Bill" — Phoebe James had been telling about something that had happened when she was lecturing in Kansas City, and they had all been listening, amused. The servant's message had been an interruption. But, if annoyed at the interruption, Ingraham had recovered himself quickly. He had thanked the man in the white coat,

34

and had picked up Mrs. James's story and handed it back to her. Only after she had finished had he said that he had to make a telephone call, and gone off to make it. He had been unhurried, suave, not then "startled." He had been gone about five minutes, perhaps ten, and had rejoined them, and made no further mention of the call.

It had been some time later — perhaps half an hour later — that Nan Schaeffer had looked at the watch on her wrist and had said, "Goodness. I'd no idea. I've really got to get away." There had then been such mutual, and conventional, expressions of esteem as are used at partings, and Nan Schaeffer had gone, Webb with her. But, as they discovered later, while themselves looking for a hostess to thank, with her only toward the door, not through it. Webb was still there, drink in hand, talking to two women and another man. Catching their eyes over the heads of others — "he's the height people ought to be in crowds," Pam said — Reginald Webb had lifted a glass toward them. He had been there when, finally, they left, to a reproachful "*Darlings! Must* you?" from Margaret.

"Then?"

Then the four of them — Ingraham and Phoebe James; the Norths — had stood in front of the apartment house and waved at taxicabs, and while they waited for a cab to condescend, it had been Ingraham who had said, "Why don't we all have dinner together. Unless you're tied up?" The last was to the Norths.

"We weren't. We'd been going out some-where anyway, because you never know about cocktail parties and it isn't fair to Martha. And we've always liked Forbes — not just as a lawyer — and Mrs. James is charming and —"

"And," Jerry said, "we'd got started. You know how it is."

They had gone to a mid-town restaurant suggested by Ingraham; described by him, during a short cab ride, as a place he often lunched, but which he thought even better at the dinner hour. "Also," he had said, "it won't be crowded."

It had not been. Perhaps a dozen tables, out of several times as many, had been occupied. But, the restaurant had not seemed, as res-taurants sometimes do under such circum-stances, at all deserted, at all dreary. The atmosphere had been relaxed, leisurely.

"For one thing," Jerry said, "the tables are far enough apart. Some of these places —"

They had had new drinks, and better ones. "The whole damn time at the party," Jerry said, "I got two and a half cocktails, not count-

36

ing the half down my sleeve."

Pam realized, now thinking back to the evening before, that she had noticed the couple at a side table, half way back in the restaurant, as the four of them were being seated near the front. But she had noticed them only absently, during that hardly conscious survey most people make on entering an unfamiliar restaurant. She did not think that Ingraham, who was first screened from them by the maitre d' and afterward sat with his back to the couple, had at first noticed them at all.

Certainly he had seemed surprised, and oddly intent when, while he and the Norths and Mrs. James sipped drinks, waited for oysters, the two had left the restaurant and, leaving it, passed close to the four at the table. Ingraham had been speaking, he stopped in mid-word. They all, as he did, looked at the backs of a slight blond girl, whose hair was a silvery cap, and a tall, thin man with black hair who walked close behind her and, as he followed her, appeared to continue a conversation which, if to be judged by his attitude, was of importance. The girl, assuming she listened, gave no sign of it, but walked away steadily, with the man behind her. She walked stiffly.

It looked like the end of an argument, or perhaps like the middle of one and Pam thought, "They've had a tiff; they're both upset" and then became conscious of the intentness with which Forbes Ingraham was looking after them. It was several seconds before Ingraham appeared aware of the silence he had caused, and then that Pam, and Mrs. James too, had turned to look at him.

"People from the office," he said. "Didn't realize they were —" But that he did not finish. Instead, he took up what he had been saying previously — seemed, indeed, to resume with the half finished word, so smoothly was the transition made.

"Tall, dark man," Weigand said, when he had heard this much. "Blond girl. That'd be Cuyler — Francis Cuyler. The girl's a stenographer — Phyllis something." He turned to Mullins in a corner of the office.

"Moore," Mullins said. "Haven't talked to her yet."

"We've talked very little to any of them," Bill Weigand told the Norths. "Starting with you, since you turned up." He gestured around the office in which they sat, with the furious wind rattling at the window. "This is Cuyler's," he said, of the office. "Go on, Pam."

"I could see the table they'd been at," Pam said. "A waiter came up with cups and a pot of coffee, and looked surprised. Then he

38

looked at the door, but they'd gone, but apparently they'd left money for the check so he shrugged. You know how waiters shrug?"

"I never noticed that they —" Bill Weigand began, in spite of himself, and then achieved resistance. Some time it would be interesting to learn, from Pamela North, how the shrugs of waiters differed from other shrugs, as presumably they did. This was not the time. "Yes," Bill said. "You felt they had left suddenly. Without finishing?"

"Oh yes," Pam said. "When she saw Forbes was there, probably. She was sitting so she could see him."

"I don't —" Jerry began, and ran a hand through his hair.

"Because of the way he — Forbes, I mean — looked at them, of course," Pam said. "What else?"

"I don't know," Jerry said, feeling, at once, that he should, and that there was something wrong with it — *post hoc ergo propter hoc,* possibly. Or, Jerry decided, a little desperately, the other way around.

After that, Pam said, they had eaten and had been waiting for dessert when the second interruption came.

"But I don't know what any of this has to do —" Pam said, and was stopped by Bill Weigand's gesture; said, "Oh, all right."

The maitre d' had come to the table, apologized for interrupting, said that a gentleman at the bar would like to see Mr. Ingraham. Ingraham had stood up, asking that they excuse him, and followed the maitre d' to the small bar at one side of the entrance to the dining area. There he had joined a tall man, who evidently awaited him, sitting on one of the stools.

"A big man, in his sixties, probably," Pam said. "He had gray hair — iron gray, they call it, although —" This time Pam stopped her own digression. "Red face and a very long jaw and he wore a blue suit that was too tight across the shoulders. Of course, I didn't want to stare."

"No," Jerry said. "Of course not, darling."

"I never," Pam said, "understand how people can just not be interested. Especially when things are so interesting."

Ingraham had talked with the man at the bar for perhaps five minutes. The big man had gone, then, and as he turned away, Ingraham had put a hand briefly on the man's shoulder, in a gesture which might have been one of encouragement. Ingraham had returned to the table, then, and there had been no further interruptions. After dinner, the Norths had gone home and, after a suitable lapse of time, to bed.

"The man at the bar," Bill Weigand said. "Describe him again, will you?" Pam described him again. Weigand's eyes narrowed; he nodded his head; he said it was interesting.

"Sounds like Matt Halpern," he said. "He was a client of Ingraham's. We've found that out."

"Halpern?" Pam repeated. "Oh, the labor czar."

He had been called that, Bill agreed. At the moment, he appeared to be a czar facing revolution, which is a common lot of czars. He was also a czar under indictment for misappropriation of union funds.

"And a client of Ingraham's?" Jerry North said, disbelief in his voice. "I never knew Forbes took on that sort of thing."

Apparently he had, this time, Bill told them. Why — well, they would try to find out. Particularly since Halpern seemed to have become a dangerous associate.

"Somebody tried to kill him around midnight last night," Bill told them. "Fired shots out of a car, into his, and, as the newspapers say, 'sped off.' Missed Halpern. Wounded a man with him, not seriously." Unexpectedly, Bill Weigand smiled, with some amusement. "Private cop," he said. "Named Mallet. Presumably a bodyguard for Halpern. But — Mallet was down on his hands and knees on the car floor a second after the first shot. A bullet ricocheted and hit him in the — well, the area most prominent in his position. Very sad case."

"Mallet?" Pam said. "Haven't I read about him somewhere?"

"I hope not, Pamela," Bill Weigand said.

Weigand stood, then, and thanked them, and promised to keep in touch — a promise which, over the years, had become inevitable — and opened the office door. Pamela started through it, and then drew back and said, in a voice suddenly very small, not quite certain, that she thought they might wait a minute. Bill looked out, and nodded, and closed the door.

Men were carrying the body of Forbes Ingraham from his big office where, at ten minutes after eleven that morning, he had been found dead. He had been shot once in the forehead, from close range. He had fallen forward on his desk, and his blood had flowed onto the yellow pad which was always there, rendering indecipherable whatever he might have written on it in his neat, small script.

The Norths, coming at noon to sign their wills, had found Acting Captain William Weigand, Homicide Squad, Manhattan West, already there — Weigand and many others, from the precinct, the police laboratory, the

District Attorney's office. By then they were all convinced that, although Forbes Ingraham might conceivably have fired the bullet into his own head, he had not done so, seemingly having lacked a weapon. Nowhere in the suite of offices was a weapon to be found, and this was to be expected. It was murder, and almost at once took on the appearance of murder most obscure.

Now Pam and Jerry North waited, and again Pam clasped her hands together, since they persisted in shaking. When they had waited long enough, Bill Weigand investigated, and went with them out of Francis Cuyler's office and through the corridor and the reception room. Mary Burton lay on the sofa in the reception room. She was very white. Bill watched them go, and turned back. He said to Mullins, "Well, let's see what it looks like."

It took them time, talking, one by one, to the people who had been in the office that morning — and who had heard no shot from Ingraham's sound-proofed office. All had been talked to earlier by detectives from the precinct, briefly by the assistant district attorney from the Homicide Bureau. They had, by and large, agreed on the facts — on the externals of the facts. Since the facts did not lead immediately to a conclusion, the assistant district attorney had gone elsewhere, leaving spade work to the police — which meant, in the first instance, to Homicide, West, which meant to Weigand, Mullins assisting — and, if developments required, some hundreds more assisting too.

Now they talked to Reginald Webb, surviving partner of Schaeffer, Ingraham and Webb; to Francis Cuyler, tall and dark, pawing black hair from a white face, an associate of the firm; to Saul Karn, five feet tall, precise, gesturing with rimless glasses to emphasize his points, and also an associate; to Phyllis Moore, pretty and white and shaken, and to Dorothy Lynch — Mrs. Dorothy Lynch — trim and competent, and showing no emotion; to Mary Burton — Mrs. Mary Burton — middle-aged and long-faced, insisting she was quite all right, holding a damp wad of handkerchief to red eyes.

Mrs. Burton, of all of them, had the most immediate reason to be near shock. She had found Ingraham's body. Remembering, she had made a low, moaning sound and covered her face with her hands. She had lifted her long face after a moment, and said, in a choked voice, that she was very sorry — that it had been a terrible shock.

In the end, she told the most of it, and her version was not substantially changed by any of the others.

She, Mary Burton, senior of the clerical force, had reached the office at nine. Precisely at nine. Mrs. Lynch had been a few minutes late; Phyllis Moore a few moments later still. Cuyler had come in at a little after nine-thirty; Karn immediately after him. Reginald Webb had arrived at about ten and had called almost at once for Mrs. Lynch and the morning mail. All these arrivals were as customary; there was, at the beginning, nothing to indicate that Tuesday, February 9, was to be different from any other day.

But then Forbes Ingraham had arrived at ten-thirty, and that was a little unexpected, being half an hour before his usual time. He had said "good morning" to Mary through the information window, as he usually did.

"And seemed as usual?"

"Yes. Oh yes." She dabbed at her eyes.

Ingraham had gone on into his office and, after a brief lapse of time — "I always waited until he had time to get settled" — Mary had called him on the telephone and given the day's schedule. His first appointment was at eleven, and with Matthew Halpern. "The labor leader, you know. The firm was representing him."

"Right," Bill Weigand said. "Go on, Mrs. Burton. Then?"

Forbes Ingraham had thanked her; had

asked about her health, and how things were on Staten Island. (Things had been cold that morning — cold and blustery.) He had hung up, then.

But, about five minutes later, which would have made it about a quarter of eleven, Ingraham had called the switchboard back and this time he had asked for an outside line. And that had been strange, almost unprecedented. "He always asked me, or sometimes one of the others, to get whoever he wanted, but this time — it was — I don't know — almost as if he didn't —" She did not finish this, or need to. Forbes Ingraham's last telephone call had been a secret one — too secret to be shared with Mary Burton. "Almost as if he didn't trust me," she might have said, been going to say. She dabbed at her eyes.

"You don't know who he called, then?"

"Of course not. How could I?"

Bill Weigand could think of a way, but did not mention it. Mary Burton was, he decided, not then in any condition to consider a suggestion that she might have listened at the switchboard.

Ingraham's call had been short. She had supposed that he had not found available the person with whom he had wished to speak.

"You and Miss Moore were still in the office? I mean, the office you share?"

46

She shook her head at that. It had been, she thought, a few minutes before Mr. Ingraham asked for the outside line that Mr. Cuyler had had Miss Moore sent in to take dictation. She would have been alone, unless — "I don't remember whether Eddie was here then. Mr. Karn sent him out on an errand, but I don't remember whether it was then or later. He's the office boy."

Bill Weigand nodded.

Mr. Halpern had been a few minutes late for his appointment — five minutes late, perhaps a little more. He had apologized; Mary had told him that she was sure it wouldn't matter, and then she would let Mr. Ingraham know he was there.

"Halpern was alone?"

"Why — yes. At least, I didn't —"

"Right," Bill said. "Then?"

She had telephoned Forbes Ingraham. And the telephone had not been answered. She had tried again, and had still not been answered. She had assumed the telephone was not ringing properly.

"Then —" she said, and once more covered her face with her hands, and once more Weigand and Mullins, sitting with her in Cuyler's office, waited.

Then she had gone into Mr. Ingraham's office, knocking first and receiving no reply; still

47

assuming that something must have happened to the telephone.

"You went through the reception room? And the library?"

She had not gone through the reception room; she had only crossed the corridor, going through a door from the clerical office and then through one, directly opposite, into the larger office where she had found Forbes Ingraham dead.

"He was — it was —" she said, and seemingly could not go on. She was told she need not. The body had been untouched when Weigand arrived. Ingraham had, apparently, been leaning forward in his chair, toward the desk; possibly talking to someone who stood on the other side of the desk, and may have leaned toward him. When he was shot, in the middle of the forehead, with a bullet from, it appeared, a thirty-two calibre revolver — they did not have the bullet, yet — he had slumped forward on the desk, his head on the blotter, on the yellow pad. His right arm rested on the desk, his left hung beside him. He had, the assistant medical examiner assumed, lost consciousness so near instantly as to make no difference; he had almost certainly been dead in seconds. Except to fall forward, he apparently had not moved after he was shot.

Mary Burton had screamed, and screamed again, and then run clumsily out of the office by the door which led to the library, and cried for help — cried that something had happened to Mr. Ingraham, that he was "hurt — terribly hurt!" She did not remember what she had said, but others remembered it so. Webb had run from his office across the library; Cuyler from his into the corridor which separated library from reception room. Saul Karn had come, but less rapidly.

And at some point during this confusion, unnoticed in the confusion, Matthew Halpern had walked out. No one admitted knowing when, or being able to guess why. Mrs. Burton was sure that he had been there from a few minutes after eleven until, failing to get an answer to her telephone call, she had gone into Ingraham's office. After that, she was sure of nothing about him, nor were the others. He had, apparently, been in the reception room only five minutes, perhaps ten.

No one had heard the shot which killed Ingraham, or would admit to having heard it. With the sound-proofing of the office, this was possible, although it still bore looking into. When Mary Burton had gone into the office, one of the big windows had been partly open, so that street noises entered. If an explosion had, dimly, been audible outside Ingraham's office, it might have been dismissed — subconsciously dismissed — as a truck backfire.

When Mrs. Burton screamed, Webb and Mrs. Lynch had been working in his office; Cuyler and Miss Moore in his. Karn had been alone in his. Phyllis Moore had been in Cuyler's office for about fifteen minutes. Before that, he had been alone there. She had been in the library. Webb and Mrs. Lynch had been at work longer, but not without interruption. He had got a long distance telephone call, which promised to take some time — and did. During it, Mrs. Lynch had first gone to the file room to get certain papers he wanted; then, taking advantage of the break, briefly out of the office and down the outside corridor to the women's toilet. Webb had, they both agreed, been finishing his conversation when she returned. She was back, they both guessed, although neither could be sure, at about eleven.

It would have been possible for any of the five, if their denials were disregarded, to go into Ingraham's office unnoticed. Mary Burton could have seen anyone who went along the corridor, and through the library, if she had been looking in that direction from the information window. She did not remember that she had been, at least until Halpern arrived, and then only briefly.

It was not, Weigand had begun to suspect by then, going to be one of those direct cases, agreeably supplied with physical clues, which Deputy Chief Inspector Artemus O'Malley so much admired, and which Sergeant Mullins admired equally — to which Weigand had, certainly no objection. The slug might have usable markings, when got out of Ingraham's head; more probably, it would have been damaged by the bone it had damaged irreparably. They had not, as yet, turned up the gun. They did not seem, again at the moment, to be on their way to establishing anything like exclusive opportunity. They had found plenty of fingerprints, but none which signed confessions, or indicated anything with any clarity.

And they knew by then that there was another entrance to Ingraham's office, and that it quite possibly had been used by his murderer.

The office had three doors — one from the library, commonly used by clients; one from the corridor, used by the stenographic people; a third, opposite the library door, which had been used, presumably, most often by the late Samuel Schaeffer and the now late Forbes Ingraham. It opened from one office into the other.

This door was unlocked when the police tried it, after the knob had been dusted for prints. A precinct man went through it first, and into another large office which had an atmosphere of settled non-occupancy. This office, also, had three doors — one from the corridor; the one through which the precinct man went out of Ingraham's office and, directly across from it, a door leading —

Arranging that the fingerprint men dust ahead of him, the precinct man had discovered where it led. He had been surprised. It led out.

It led into a wide corridor, evidently a public one, and so provided an entirely separate — and unadvertised — entrance to the offices of Schaeffer, Ingraham and Webb. It did, exploration disclosed, more than this — through a doorway, past an open, metal fire-door, it led into the adjacent building and, after a turning, to two elevators. (It was subsequently discovered that the party wall between two similarly elderly and dignified buildings had been so pierced at every floor level when, a good many years before, they had come under common management.)

The knobs on the door between Ingraham's office and that of his late partner, the knobs on the door which led to the outer corridor — on none of these four knobs was there any fingerprint whatever. The door to the building corridor was locked. The inter-office door was not.

With all this Mullins, hearing of it, had been pleased. They knew something, anyway — the killer could have come and gone through Schaeffer's office, wiping doorknobs as he left. Mullins was then so close to purring that Weigand hesitated to mention the obvious — that this might be appearance, not truth; that, specifically, anyone, however he had in fact entered Ingraham's office, might take the trouble to wipe off knobs, so providing that element of misdirection understandably prized by murderers.

It was then, although the Norths were not actually yet in it — being only names on an engagement record — that Mullins decided it was another screwy one, and so remarked.

"Screwy?" Weigand repeated. "Isn't porous more like it, sergeant?"

Either was bad enough, Mullins said. And Artie would not like it.

"Unless it's Halpern," Mullins added. "Artie'll like Halpern fine."

Bill Weigand wasn't sure he didn't like Matthew Halpern fine himself. It appeared that violence had begun to build up about Halpern, and that was always interesting. They would —

The telephone rang on the desk in the office from which Francis Cuyler had now been for some time excluded. Weigand answered it, said, "Yes," said, "Put him on," said, "Yes, counsellor," and listened for more than a minute.

"Right," he said, then. "Thanks for passing it on. It can be very helpful."

He put the receiver back and looked at it.

"The call Ingraham made," he said after a moment, "was to District Attorney Sumner. It was to arrange an appointment for this afternoon. It went through at about ten forty-five. But — the appointment wasn't made. Ingraham started to go into details and interrupted himself. He said, 'Can I call you back in about half an hour?' The D.A. was just saying 'Sure, Forbes' when Ingraham hung up. Seemed hurried. So —"

"Somebody came in," Mullins said.

"Right," Bill Weigand said. "I'd think so, sergeant. Enter, a murderer."

III

When Pam and Jerry North have lunch together they commonly spend more time about it than they plan to, or than is for any practical purpose necessary. Such luncheons, usually for no especial reason, tend to become minor celebrations — the signing of wills, after long consideration and much postponement, might well have provided occasion for celebration, or the fact that it was Tuesday. But they had not signed wills, and it was anything but a good Tuesday, for this time a friend had died.

Forbes Ingraham had not been a close friend, but he had been a pleasant one of rather long standing. Each in his own way was thinking of Forbes Ingraham, and not of the manner of his death, as they stood on a windy sidewalk in front of the elderly, and most dignified, office building and waved at passing taxicabs. It was Pam who suggested they forego the luncheon they had planned; Pam who said it wouldn't seem right, somehow, because, in

55

spite of themselves, they would enjoy it. The logic might be contested, Jerry thought, and smiled down at her — the logic but not the spirit.

So the cab, when one answered, dropped Jerry at his office, which (he thought) was certainly where he ought to be if things were to be in any sense cleaned up for holiday, and took Pam home. It would, she decided there, be a good afternoon to balance her bank statement. That should keep her mind off things. She, therefore, shut herself away from cats, who were made furious — Martini clawed at the very best chair, in reprisal — provided herself with abundance of scratch paper and went at it. If she could only, she was thinking in ten minutes, remember to do them as soon as they came, instead of a week afterward when they were harder —

In half an hour, she had struck a balance, but it was evidently not the right balance. It had better not be. She must, she decided, be subtracting the wrong thing from the other thing, or perhaps adding a deposit to a withdrawal. Pam thought, with care, slowly. You take your present balance, and add to it the sum of the checks that haven't gone through, and that will be what the bank says the present balance is, if you add deposits that haven't — Was that really the right way? The way she had done it the month before, when it really had balanced, if you didn't count the odd cents and took into account the deficit left over from the month before? Or was it better to deduct the outstanding checks from the balance the bank had decided on and then subtract the deposits — No, surely you didn't *subtract* deposits. If you added what the check book showed to what —

"This," Pam North said aloud, "is perfectly ridiculous. I've done this dozens of times. You take what doesn't show in the book and add it to what doesn't show in the statement and then —" Pam leaned back. She put the pencil in her mouth and chewed it absently. The funny thing, she thought, is that I've always rather *liked* the taste of lead pencil since I was a little girl. Only there was that awful time when it was an indelible pencil. I'll just keep cool and add all the ones that are out to what the book shows is in and then —

She did this. She now apparently had in the account four hundred and sixty-six dollars and the cents — but forget the cents — less than she had thought she had. This was extremely depressing. If it was going to stay this way, it would be silly of them to try to go to Florida. Of course, they weren't going to go on this account, but still —

Sometimes when you added down, you got

57

an entirely different answer than if you added up. The thing to do was to start over entirely, because otherwise you made the same mistakes again. Pam copied figures into a column, being very careful to keep the decimal points in a straight line, because if you started adding the cents in with the dollars it was hopeless. (She had done that once and come up with a bonanza of nearly a thousand dollars, but Jerry had checked her figures and lost the money. This had depressed both of them.) "And carry three," Pam said, "and nine is twelve and six is eighteen and seven is twenty-three and —"

It came out better. It came out too much better. Now she had a hundred and twelve dollars (and the cents) *more* than she ought to have. It was —

"Damn!" Pam North said. "If it takes all afternoon I'll —"

But then the telephone on her desk rang.

Phoebe James's voice had velvet in it. She had heard only an hour before about this awful thing that had happened — about Forbes. The richly soft voice shook then. "About Forbes," Phoebe James repeated, and it was as if she repeated the name to make herself believe. "You were friends of his, weren't you? You and your husband?"

"Yes," Pam said. "It is hard to believe. When only last night —" She did not finish.

She felt that Mrs. James merely waited, did not listen.

"Can you," Mrs, James said, "is there any chance you can — have tea with me this afternoon? I —" She stopped. "I want to see you," she said. "You and Mr. North."

"Why —" Pam said.

"Please. If you possibly can. About five?"

"Yes," Pam said. "I think so. I'm almost sure, really. Unless Jerry can't get away."

"Try. Please try. I'm at the Westminster. In East Fifty-first, you know? Tell your husband it's — I'd like to see you very much."

Pam looked at the telephone for a moment after she had replaced the receiver. She had thought they would be out of this one, except for what Bill told them; except for what, and that so without pertinence, they had already told Bill. But the urgency in Phoebe James's beautiful voice —

Pam dialed North Books, Inc.; got Jerry; heard him say, "Now listen, Pam —" finally heard him say, "All right, I suppose so. I'll meet you there. I had thought —"

"Good," Pam said. "In the lobby."

She replaced the receiver, and was confronted with columns of figures. She shook her head; she put the pencil back into her mouth, and chewed it gently. She said, "Oh well," and made a new listing of the checks which had not cleared. She added this column until, on two additions, she got the same total. She subtracted the sum so arrived at from the balance shown on the statement. She drew a double line across the stub sheet in her check book, so wiping out all that had gone before. Below the double line she entered the new balance, dating it.

"Let them," Pam North said, "have it their way." As, she added to herself, they will in any case; as they always do.

She spent time with the cats, who then were pleased with her. She lowered them from her lap, and they were no longer pleased. She went to the kitchen, and told Martha that, the way it looked, they wouldn't be home for dinner.

"You weren't home last night," Martha said. "This leg of lamb I was going to do yesterday — there's a limit to legs of lamb, Mrs. North, even in the refrigerator."

"I know," Pam said. "Why don't you take it home, Martha? Before it does?"

To this Martha said, "Yes'm," but over it she shook her head. Pam shook her own; this was no way to save for Florida, and only a few days left. Pam bathed and dressed, and now she could not make her mind forget murder. It was about that that Phoebe James wanted to see them, of course; wanted so insistently to see them. She took a cab to the

Westminster, which is a residential hotel of some elegance. She was a few minutes early, but Jerry was not appreciably late. He looked, however, like a man who has spent a day at the office and for this, seeing Pam — who looked like a lady dressed for tea, although hatlessly — apologized mildly. He also said that it would be nice to have a little time at home, some time.

They were announced, rode up in an elevator which (a little gratuitously Pam thought) provided a cushioned bench. They went along a carpeted corridor and rang the indicated bell, which responded musically with chimes. A uniformed maid opened the door for them, took their coats, preceded them across a foyer into a long room. Mrs. Phoebe James, who wore a black dress, and was very grave, came toward them, down the room. She's very handsome, Pam North thought. The velvet voice said it was wonderful of them to have come. "I know I'm imposing on you," Phoebe James said, and merely smiled and shook her head slightly when this was denied. She said that she was having tea, but that there were alternatives; said she knew most people didn't expect tea when asked to tea; said, "Forbes keeps telling me —" and put a long-fingered brown hand up so that the fingers for an instant covered her eyes. She swallowed. She

61

said, then, "I'm sorry."

"I'd love tea," Pam North said, quickly.

"I —" Jerry said, and just perceptibly hesitated.

"Wouldn't," Phoebe James said, and suggested whiskey. Or a cocktail? Jerry, so urged, chose a martini. Mrs. James rang and they waited. She rose from a deep chair — all the chairs were deep, as the carpet was deep. The apartment inclined to wrap itself around its occupants. She walked to a window and said that they must see her view, and they saw her view, which was New York from height, lighted and so spectacular. "People are so much smaller," Phoebe James said, and turned away as the maid brought tea, a pitcher holding more than one martini, a chilled glass. "Thank you, dear," Phoebe James said, and looked at the tray, found it complete. "We'll ring if there's anything more."

She poured tea, then, not hurrying as the maid walked the long length of the room and out of it. She handed a cup to Pam, watched while Jerry filled his glass. She put her own cup down on a little table, and did not drink from it.

"Forbes and I were in love," she said, then, and spoke as if the sentence, in its simplicity, had for some time been formed in her mind. She did not look at them when she spoke, but did so immediately she had spoken.

"It's an odd thing to say to people who are almost strangers," she said. "I assume a great deal. Demand a great deal." She looked from one to the other. Then she smiled faintly. "I wouldn't have a character say it that way," she said. "Not so — barely. I'd write in — oh, little gasps. Little verbal gasps." She looked directly at Jerry. "You know," she told him. He nodded his head.

"Only," she said, "it was as simple as that — as final. I'm — well, I'm almost fifty." She shook her head. "I'm quite fifty," she said. "Forbes was older, a few years older. I've been married twice. And so — Forbes and I were in love. And now it's a story I tell to strangers."

She sipped from her teacup, finally.

"A story told to strangers," she repeated. "That would make a title, wouldn't it? Probably it has." She put the cup down, very gently. She said, "Damn! I — I always listen to the words. It's a trick of the trade. But I wouldn't have written it the way it was. Lovers — they're always young, aren't they? In their twenties, or thirties at most. Or very dewy and in their 'teens and hesitant — so prettily hesitant, so God-damn hesitant. People in their fifties wear slippers and sit by fires, and kiss each other on foreheads and worry about the younger generation." She stopped.

"I'm not very coherent," she said. "I am usually quite coherent. Your cup is empty, Mrs. North."

Pam looked at her cup. Surprisingly, it was empty. "It's dry work listening," Phoebe James said, and Pam held out the cup. As she filled it, Phoebe James's hand was entirely steady.

"Why did he die?" she said. "I have to know. You see why I have to know. All this was so you would."

"We don't know," Pam said. "How could we know, Mrs. James?"

"I want —" Mrs. James said, and sipped from her cup. "I want you to help me find out. You've found out things like this — things about murder. You've —"

"Wait," Jerry said. "We're not detectives. We're just people who —" He paused. "Who know a detective," he said. The truth, he thought uneasily, is so seldom convincing. "That's all, really," he added, weakening it further.

"I'm not," Phoebe James said, "suggesting you are for hire, Mr. North. But — I've thought recently I might change publishers and —"

"No," Jerry said. "Oh, we'd like to have you. Who wouldn't? But — no." He paused.

"Not on this basis," he said, and uneasily realized that, so, he left a door not quite closed. Or not, at any rate, quite locked.

"The police won't find out," Mrs. James said. "Or, not if it's a certain way. They — well, they won't be allowed to. Unless somebody else finds out enough to make them. I'm going to find out. If you won't help me —" She stopped. "Forbes Ingraham was your friend too," she said. "He was fond of both of you, and he wasn't fond of a great many people. Last night he was alive. He laughed, remember? He held that cigarette holder in his left hand and gestured with it in a certain way he had. He spoke in a certain way — used certain words. His mind was a kind of light. Today, somebody switched the light off. Like that — click — out." She raised her teacup, but seemed not to know she had done so, and did not drink from it. "You can't not care," she said, and spoke very slowly.

"It isn't that," Pam said. "It isn't that at all. But, what can we do? That the police —"

"I know a great many of the people Forbes knew," Phoebe James said. "I know more about them than the police can ever find out — from what he said, from what I've seen, and listened to. Even if the police tried they couldn't —"

"Wait," Jerry said. "You said something

like that a minute ago. That the police won't try. They won't be allowed to, you said. That simply isn't true. What did you mean by that, Mrs. James?"

"What is your friend?" she said. "A lieutenant? A captain?"

"Acting Captain."

"And over him, inspectors and chief inspectors and a commissioner, and over the commissioner — all the men who run the city. The men who sell protection, collect from the rackets. Suppose your friend is the most honest cop who ever lived. You think he can't be stopped? Taken off the case? Sent to some sort of Siberia? So that it can all be covered up."

"What?" Jerry said. "What do you think they'd want covered up?"

(Whatever we say, we're getting into it, Pam North thought. And — she knows it. Pam considered. I guess, she thought, we're pushovers at heart. Unconsciously, she sighed.)

"Can't I get some hot tea?" Phoebe James said. "Because — you'll at least listen. I know you'll listen."

"Well," Pam North said, and looked at Jerry. "I think this time I'll have a drink, Mrs. James. A martini, I guess."

The maid was rung for, instructed.

"Have you," Phoebe James said, "heard of a man named Matthew Halpern? A labor leader? He's been indicted for embezzling union funds. Last night at the restaurant, he was the man Forbes saw at the bar." She looked at them. "You did know that?" she said.

"We heard that today," Pam said. "Bill Weigand told us. He's our detective."

"Forbes was Halpern's attorney. Forbes talked about it to me. Generally — about what it meant, why he got into it. Because, it was outside his usual practice, of course. His usual practice — well, it was with people like me. That's how we met. But you know that, Mr. North. Everybody like us knew that."

"Yes."

"Mr. Halpern is being framed," Mrs. James said. "Forbes was certain of that. By racketeers — gangsters, really — who are trying to take over the union. So they can turn it into a racket. And — Forbes has been digging into it. I don't know what he's found out. He didn't tell me that. Perhaps he found out too much and —"

The maid returned. Phoebe James waited until she had gone out again.

"Perhaps what he found out was dangerous," Mrs. James said. "I don't know. If he could manage it, Forbes would have done whatever he could to break up the racket. If men like that killed him, they'll have protection. The police will protect them. Things are done that way. If —"

"Not," Pam North said, "by Bill Weigand. If you think —"

"An acting captain," Phoebe James said. "Just an acting captain. What —"

Chimes sounded melodiously. The maid appeared at the far end of the room, but Phoebe James said, "Never mind, dear," and went into the foyer. She returned at once, not alone. Nan Schaeffer wore the mink still, loose on her shoulders. She was not surprised to find the Norths there. She held out a hand to Pam, then to Jerry; she maintained the fiction of a smile on stiff lips. This was prearranged, Pam thought; Mrs. James was very sure of us.

"The four of us," Phoebe James said. "The four of us can —"

The office was small and bare and hot; the hot air smelled and tasted of dust. If, as charged, money was leaking from the union treasury into Matthew Halpern's private pocket, he was using none of it to provide amenities — here, at any rate. He sat at a plain desk, in a wooden chair, on a felt pad; he was coatless, his shirt open, showing a corded neck.

"I don't know anything about it," he said, not for the first time. "You won't get anything different."

His voice had harshness in it, as if it had long been strained. He had shouted, Bill Weigand thought, in too many echoing halls, perhaps too often in damp winds on street corners. Fog rasped in his voice.

"You were there, Mr. Halpern," Bill Weigand said. "When you heard Mr. Ingraham had been shot, you got out in a hurry."

"She didn't say he was shot," Halpern said. "Something about his being hurt. Hurt bad."

"All right," Bill said. "All the more reason. You didn't stay around to see if you could help."

"There were plenty without me," Halpern said.

Bill waited.

"O.K.," Halpern said. "I didn't want to get mixed up in anything. A guy gets hurt, chances are somebody hurt him. A guy who just sits at a desk, anyway. That's the way I figure it."

Probably, Bill Weigand thought, on the basis of experience. He nodded his head. He waited.

"I've been framed once," Halpern said.

"It didn't look good, captain."

"You think it made it look better to get out?"

"Maybe not. Maybe I moved too quick." He took a cigar out of the top drawer of his desk, bit off the end. "Want one?" he said, clearly on second thought.

"Not right now," Bill said.

"You been shot at much, captain?" Halpern asked, and flicked a kitchen match with a broad thumb nail.

"Now and then," Bill said. "Goes with the job, Mr. Halpern."

"Yeah," Halpern said. "Suppose it does. They tried to get me last night. Hear about that?"

"I heard somebody did. Yes."

"Same pack of rats thought up this other deal," Halpern said. "Guess they figured it wasn't working out right, what with Mr. Ingraham in it. Figured to hurry things up."

"If you know the men —" Bill said.

"Sure," Halpern said. "Point them out and what? Twenty guys show up and say they was all playing tiddlywinks. Anyhow, I didn't. Didn't see them to know them, and wouldn't have known them anyway. Just who hired them. They ain't nice boys, captain. They're racket boys. Somebody gets in the way — bang!"

"You think Mr. Ingraham might have got in the way."

Halpern looked at Bill Weigand with eyes narrowed in his broad, roughly reddened face.

"See that, huh?" he said. "Could be. Could be they figured he was getting something on them. Maybe he was — maybe we both were."

"You thought of that this morning? Thought it was a good place to get out of?"

"Could be," Halpern said. "No point in making it too easy for the rats. Like the fellow says."

Bill Weigand waited to hear what the fellow said. He was not enlightened.

"Tell you what," Halpern said. "I'll give you the setup. You want to listen? Can't make you believe it, but you want to listen?"

"Well," Bill Weigand said, "that's what I came for, isn't it?"

He didn't, Halpern said, have to take his word for it. But this was the way it was — did the captain know much about the union?

"Go ahead."

It was a union of men who weren't particularly skilled. They didn't get the wages of skilled workers. They got better wages now than they had ten years ago. That was about all anybody could say. Halpern had helped organize the union, he had been its president for the past ten years. "I make a little more than the boys. Not a hell of a lot more." The union was, now, affiliated with the Federation. It had a contract; it had another contract coming up for negotiation. "We're getting the squeeze, the way things are. More than most." But to take the squeeze off, to bargain for what they could get, that was what the union was for — what Halpern and the other officers were paid for.

Since the signing of the previous contract, they had slowly been building up funds to be used if, the next time, they "had trouble."

"What these newspaper guys call a 'war chest,' " Halpern said.

The money came slowly, out of low wages. It hadn't built fast; it wasn't large yet.

"Year ago, maybe year and a half, these rats tried to move in. Wanted to get a shakedown going. I knew it and some of the others. Some of the boys they fooled — got 'em believing I was too old for the job, not tough enough with the bosses. That sort of crap. Trouble was, they didn't get enough of 'em thinking that. So they pull this frame."

A shortage appeared in the union funds. Halpern did not deny that; he admitted he could not put his finger on the men responsible. He admitted, too, that they had made it look bad. "Looked like I'd been milking the fund. Misappropriation of union funds, they call it. Grand larceny, the indictment says. They hang it on me, they get me out, they take over."

Forbes Ingraham was representing Halpern. He had men going into it. He —

"Wait a minute," Weigand said. "Why Ingraham? It's out of his line. Didn't you know that?"

Halpern had not, he said, known anything about Forbes Ingraham, one way or another — not at first. Ingraham had got in touch with him, indirectly. "First I thought he was just a shyster. Kind of ambulance chaser, like the fellow says." But he had asked around; learned of the status of Schaeffer, Ingraham and Webb, gone to see Ingraham.

"Figured when I saw the setup it was way out of line for us. Where'd we get that kind of money?"

But he had talked to Forbes Ingraham. And, he had been told to forget about the fee.

"Seems like he just didn't like rats," Halpern said. "Said New York was his town and he didn't want rats taking it over, and you had to start somewhere. Funny sort of guy, wasn't he?"

"No fee at all?"

"That was his idea. I couldn't see it that way, so he says, all right, we could make it a hundred bucks."

"He was getting places?"

But Matthew Halpern shook his big, gray head at that. He said, "Nope," to that.

"You mean he wasn't?"

"What I mean, captain — why tell you if he was? See what I mean? These guys are in the rackets. So, they got protection. I don't say anything about you — far's I know you're an honest cop. But — you see how it is. If we got anything, we wouldn't want to tip anybody, would we?"

"I think you're making a mistake, Mr. Halpern."

"Maybe."

"Mr. Ingraham's dead."

"Yeah. The firm ain't, is it? I don't know where I stand, but could be we can pick up the pieces."

"If the pieces are around, these 'rats' you think killed Ingraham didn't get anywhere, did they?"

"Listen," Halpern said. "I don't know who killed Ingraham. Maybe some babe got jealous. All I know is what I was doing there. That's what you wanted to know, ain't it."

"Right," Bill said.

"O.K. I got there about eleven, maybe a few minutes after. This dame went in to tell Ingraham I was there and comes running

74

out, saying he's hurt. I left. I wasn't out of that place you wait in."

"Not then," Bill said.

Halpern looked at him.

"Mr. Ingraham probably was dead when you went in," Bill Weigand told him. "Probably had been for fifteen minutes or so."

Halpern stood up behind the desk. He was a very big man; he had been a powerful one. He still was powerful enough.

"You getting at something?" he asked, and the rasp was rougher in his voice.

"There is another way into the offices," Weigand said. "You didn't know that, Mr. Halpern?"

"Through the —" Halpern began, and stopped.

"Right," Bill said. "Through the other office — the one Mr. Schaeffer occupied before his death. You did know about that, apparently."

"All right," Halpern said. "Sure. We went back there one evening — Ingraham and me — to look at some stuff I'd — to look at some stuff. He took me in what he called the back way." The stub of the cigar moved in powerful teeth. "So what?" Halpern asked.

Bill Weigand stood up then. He said he didn't know what. Except what was obvious. He supposed obvious to Mr. Halpern. Whoever killed Forbes Ingraham could have got to him through the other office. So — being in the reception room when his body was found didn't mean anything.

"You want to pin this on me?"

"On whoever did it, Mr. Halpern."

Halpern glared at him, and was advised to take it easy.

"You got it wrong," Halpern said. "Maybe that's the way you want to get it? Maybe these rats are pals of yours?"

"No," Bill said. "Not of mine, Mr. Halpern. No killer is."

"O.K.," Halpern said. "That sounds swell, captain. Why'd I want to knock Ingraham off? We was working together to get these rats. So — how do you figure?"

"I don't," Bill said. "Not yet. But I don't know what he found out, do I?"

Halpern waited. His face was very red, angry.

"It could be," Bill Weigand said, "that he found out the wrong thing. Not what he was supposed to find out. Since he was your attorney, it would have been confidential, under the rules. But you didn't know him very well, you say. Maybe —"

"Listen," Halpern said, and spoke very loudly. "You going to take me in?"

Weigand shook his head.

"Then suppose you get the hell out of here," Halpern said.

The office was Halpern's. Weigand left him in it.

IV

It was not to be the four of them, not as Phoebe James seemed to mean. Jerry had tried to make that clear; he went to pains to make it clearer. Murder was for the police, not for amateurs. They, he and Pam, were not even amateurs. They were bystanders. If they sometimes got involved, it was as bystanders.

"Well —" Pam said, slowly.

Jerry shook his head at her. There was no "well" about it. If, as bystanders, they happened on anything that might help, they took what they had happened on to the police — specifically, to Bill Weigand. They always had, always would. He looked at Pamela.

"Of course," Pam said. "Always. Nothing behind anybody's back."

"You trust this Weigand," Phoebe James said. She looked at Nan Schaeffer. She said, "They know him, Nan. Perhaps we —" She waited. She seemed to hand the decision to the younger woman.

78

Nan Schaeffer absently stroked the mink which lay softly on the arm of her chair. It was as if, Pam North thought, she expected response, perhaps a purr. But minks do not purr. That much, at any rate, Pam knew of them.

"I don't know," Nan Schaeffer said, finally. "If only Sam —" She shook her head. There was uncertainty on regular features, to which, Pam thought, uncertainty was commonly a stranger. "Sam would know what we ought to do."

She looked up from the coat, at the Norths. "There's no use saying that," she said. "Sam isn't here. Forbes isn't here." She paused again. "Forbes wasn't going to the police," she said. "He was going beyond them, to the district attorney. Mr. Sumner. He didn't trust the police. Not in a thing like this."

She sat with her chin up; she challenged them. Phoebe James glanced at the Norths; then turned toward Nan, her expression intent.

"I talked to him yesterday," she said. "Yesterday afternoon. After you left the office, before we all met at Margaret's. You saw me there. When you went out, I was in —"

"Yes," Jerry said.

"You'll listen?"

They would listen; of course they would listen. With the understanding that —

"Oh," Nan Schaeffer said, "without prejudice. You've made that clear, Mr. North." She took a cigarette from a case, leaned forward to a lighter flame Jerry held for her; breathed smoke deeply, and exhaled it high in the air. "Forbes was preoccupied. I think he was worried about this — you've told them, Phoebe?"

"About Matthew Halpern," Phoebe James said. "A little. I — I wanted them to hear you tell it."

"He'd found out it was bigger than he'd thought it was," Nan Schaeffer said. "At least, I think so. He didn't come straight out. He often didn't, you know. You knew him that well?"

"Yes," Jerry North said.

"And of course, he couldn't. Mr. Halpern was his client, so ethics came into it. But —"

She had gone to see Forbes Ingraham the previous afternoon, at his suggestion. They talked, she said, about her late husband's estate, of which Ingraham was an executor. They talked about sums still due the estate from the firm, which Schaeffer and Ingraham had founded together years before.

"Things like that," she said. "Business things. I kept saying that I didn't have to know, wouldn't really understand, that he

80

should make any decision that had to be made. But he said I had to be told — that now I had to listen. So, I tried to. It's all — I'm afraid it doesn't seem very important to me."

"It should," Phoebe James told her, in the manner of one to whom such things were highly important. She shook her head, smiling faintly.

"I know," Nan Schaeffer said. "You're always telling me but — it's different for you. I'm no good at things like that. Anyway —"

Anyway, she had done her best to listen, and listened to the end. Then, when Forbes Ingraham finished, the animation which had been in his face as he sought words to simplify financial matters for the comprehension of his partner's widow — "I think it interested him. It was a kind of challenge" — then the animation died out. "And he looked worried," Nan Schaeffer said. "As if something which was worrying him had come back. I asked him what was the matter."

At first he said that nothing was the matter. "The way men do, when there is; when they don't want to worry you." Then he said that the Halpern matter had got rather sticky.

"That was the word he used. 'Sticky.' I said I was sorry, and was it anything he wanted to talk about? He said I ought to know better than that; that I'd been enough with lawyers to know better than that. There was nothing to talk about. It was all — what do they say. Sub something?"

"Rosa," Pam North said.

"Judice?" Jerry North said.

"That's it," Nan Schaeffer said, and nodded her head at Jerry. "Not to be talked about with outsiders. But then he said, 'There's more to it than I figured at first. Not as simple as I thought.' And then something about having to take it to the district attorney."

"Take what?" Pam asked.

Nan Schaeffer did not know, she told them. Something about the Halpern case. Something that worried Forbes Ingraham.

"That's all you remember?"

"Yes," she said. "Except —"

Her appointment had been Forbes Ingraham's last, at the office, of the day before. When they had finished, he had gone out with her. They had gone out "the back way."

The Norths shook their heads. They had not heard of the back way. Nan Schaeffer explained.

At the door which led from Schaeffer's former office to the rear corridor, Ingraham had reached around Nan Schaeffer, she told them. He had taken the knob and started to open the door and then had said, "Wait a minute," and, instead of opening the door for her to precede him, had stepped in front of her, opened the door slowly, and then, without stepping through the door, but rather by peering around it, had looked up and down the corridor. Then he had gone into the corridor and let her follow him.

"You thought —" Jerry said.

"He thought somebody might be there. I felt that, anyway."

But there had been no one. Ingraham had closed the door after them, and tried the knob, making certain the door was locked. Then they had gone out, through the "twin" building — "the Siamese twins, Sam used to call them" — and he had put her in a cab. She had gone home.

"That is," she said. "What I call that. To the East Plaza — the hotel I'm staying at since —" She looked away from them. "Well," she said, "that's it."

But it was not all of it.

"Forbes came here, then," Phoebe James said. "He —" She stopped for a moment. "We had a cup of tea and he freshened up and then we went to Margaret's. And — it's true he seemed worried. Not like himself. Preoccupied."

"About the Halpern case?" Jerry asked.

Just perceptibly, Phoebe James shrugged.

"I don't know," she said. "I didn't ask —

didn't ask anything. He was tired, I thought, and when he was tired — If there was something he wanted to tell me, he would. I — I never questioned him." She smiled, and seemed to be remembering. "I didn't need to, really," she said. "When he was worried I knew, of course, but it was the way he felt that mattered. Not *why* he felt that way. We — we never hurried each other. Only if it was something which might be, or come to be, or seem to be, a — an impingement. Like poor little Phyllis or —" And then the softly beautiful voice died out. "I didn't mean to say that," she said, after a little. "I'm afraid I was talking to myself."

"Anyway," Nan Schaeffer said, "that hasn't anything to do with it." She paused. "How could it have?"

"You don't know what we're talking about, do you?" Phoebe James said to the Norths. "I suppose — well, I suppose you'd better. You know the girl at the office — the blond girl, very pretty. Very — young?" She paused again. "So very young," she said. "Not half his age. Or mine. Oh — or mine."

She was silent for some seconds; sat with her head bent, so that the light accentuated the white streak in her brown hair. She looked her age then, Pam North thought; before, she had seemed without age.

"She fell in love with Forbes," Phoebe James said, without looking up, looking at the light on her hands, at a large, carved ring on the little finger of her left hand. "Or thought she did. When I was her age, it would have been called a crush, perhaps. I don't know what they call it now. He was — to a young woman, he must have seemed so much. Experienced, successful — complete, as young men aren't. Or most of them aren't." She shook her head. "I've written that, too," she said. "More than once. The dewy girl enamored of the older man. Mine always go back to the boy, of course. Youth calls to youth. Perhaps youth doesn't answer sometimes, but —" She paused. "I don't try to teach old readers new tricks," she said.

"Anyway —"

Anyway, the girl Phyllis had fallen in love with, or become enamored of, the older man. The older man had not reciprocated. They would think — oh, that she would have thought that; would have made herself think that, truth or not; would have been told that. They would think her naive. "But I'm not," Phoebe James said. "Oh, not for a long time."

But the situation had been, nevertheless, a mildly uncomfortable one for Forbes Ingraham. The girl was efficient; she was also a very "nice" girl. "He called her that." He

85

could have discharged her. "But that wouldn't have been fair. He thought it wouldn't." So, he had temporized — limited his contacts with her as much as he could without raising an issue; used Dorothy Lynch, particularly after Schaeffer's death, instead of Phyllis Moore.

Mrs. James deviated, here. They were not to think that Forbes had been strait-laced. There had been girls in the past. "Before we —" She did not finish. But they had not been girls working in the office. Such relationships, aside from everything else, were complications. And, she thought — thought he had thought — a little vulgar. "Although why, I don't know," she said. "And anyway —" She stopped again. She did not, she said, know why she was telling all this, since it was so far from the point. But — there had been a further complication. Francis Cuyler — "the tall dark man at the office; the rather dramatic man?" — apparently felt about Phyllis as Phyllis did about Forbes Ingraham. Youth calling to youth again. In this case, apparently not being answered. At least —

"The office triangle," she said, and then, for the first time, she laughed briefly, without mirth.

The laughter accepted a cliché of situation; one, the laughter said, which might have been Phoebe James's own. There was wryness in

86

the quick laughter. She's self-conscious about what she writes, Pam North thought. I must ask Jerry.

"You see why we — Nan and I — feel we can't trust the police," Mrs. James said. "Why —" She paused. "I'll find the one who killed Forbes," she said, and for that moment her voice was no longer soft. "Oh, I'll find him."

"No," Reginald Webb said, "I don't know why Forbes wanted an appointment with the district attorney, captain. It's not unusual for circumstances to come up which lead an attorney to want a conference."

"This isn't a firm which handles criminal cases to any extent," Bill said. "I gather that's true?"

"Except this Halpern matter. That was pretty much Forbes's own operation. I'd guess it concerned that, yes. But I'd only be guessing. Forbes might have wanted to find out —" He stopped. He shook his head.

They sat in his office, which was smaller than those which had been occupied by the two senior partners. He sat erect behind a wide desk, and he sat tall. He spoke crisply, and with emphasis. Already, he had assured Weigand that he knew nothing which might help to the solution of Forbes Ingraham's murder. Of that, his professed ignorance was no greater, and no less, than that of any of the others in the office — of long-faced Mary Burton, or of Dorothy Lynch or Phyllis Moore; of Francis Cuyler, who pushed at black hair, or the precise Saul Karn, who made his points — seemed to chop his points — with small, quick movements of his rimless glasses.

Long before, the office would normally have been closed for the day. Mary Burton would have been on a ferryboat plodding through the bay toward Staten Island; the other women on subways, or leaving them and walking through evening streets; Webb himself, Bill Weigand guessed, would have crossed Forty-fourth Street to the Harvard Club. But the lights still burned in the offices, and the staff stayed.

Webb had been left to the last in this final round of the day's questioning. The first round had established facts, as stated. Those subsequent sought to relate facts. And from each, beyond statements of fact, came more — came the less tangible things; came relationships and matters for speculation. (There was considerable violence in Francis Cuyler, particularly at any mention of the blond Miss Moore; Mrs. Burton still dabbed at red eyes; for Saul Karn, from all he showed, the death of Forbes Ingraham might have been a misplaced comma in a brief, rendering its legality

88

doubtful. He appeared to take the matter under consideration.)

Nor, now, did Reginald Webb reveal what emotions he might feel. He had seemed shocked at first; expressed, at first, that disbelief which is so often the first reaction to violence. He had made it clear that he had thought of Forbes Ingraham as a friend. But on what, under those circumstances, he presumably felt, he had closed a door, which fitted perfectly.

"You want to know what happened, how it happened," he had told Bill Weigand. "Not how I feel about it. You want evidence."

That was true enough, if by no means all the truth. Bill had accepted it.

His guesses about the reasons for Ingraham's wish to see District Attorney Sumner would not, he pointed out, be evidence. Ingraham might have had any of a dozen purposes. That Halpern was involved was, obviously, the most probable of alternatives.

"When a defense attorney wants to talk to the district attorney," Webb said now, "one thinks first of some sort of compromise. Plea to a lesser charge. But —"

Bill Weigand waited.

"I'd be surprised, in this case," Webb said. "Doesn't sound like Forbes. He was — well, he was all het up about it. You wouldn't think he would be — been around a good while, pretty calm about things, for the most part. About some things he wasn't, and this Halpern business seemed to be one of them. It's not a case I'd expect him to compromise. Still — I don't know what came up. Maybe the case fell apart when he began to look at it."

"Would anybody else know about that?"

Webb doubted it. If letters had been written, instruments prepared, one of the girls would know. Dorothy Lynch, probably; perhaps Mrs. Burton. Ingraham might even have told Mrs. Burton if there had been — well, a hitch.

"She says not," Bill told him.

It wouldn't be much help in any case, Webb said. He said, "Poor old Mary." Again, Bill Weigand waited.

"She's been around for I don't know how long," Webb said. "Before I joined the firm. Forbes was her particular chick. She used to be his secretary. Then — well, we all get older. She does seem to have got older more than most, somehow. Gets things muddled up a good deal and —" He stopped. Then he said that the captain might as well know.

"We hadn't broken it to her yet," he said. "Unless Forbes did in the last day or so. We'd decided we'd have to retire her. Full salary, Forbes insisted on that. She's got a little house on Staten Island, and a little garden — and all that sort of thing. But — well, I'd have hated to be the one to tell her. Have to now, as things stand, but now — well, it probably won't be so bad. There'll be a lot of changes. She'll recognize that. And, with Forbes gone, she probably won't care too much. But, to tell her she was too old for it — made too many mistakes — that wouldn't have been pleasant. Forbes dreaded it. But what could we do?"

Bill Weigand nodded his head to that. He said that what Webb had just said brought up another point. Probably not germane. But still —

"We have to poke around," Bill Weigand said. "Find out all people are willing to tell us. What happens to the firm now, Mr. Webb?"

"Not much left of Schaeffer, Ingraham and Webb, is there?" Reginald Webb said. "The last survivor. I don't mind telling you. I haven't decided. I may try to get somebody else to come in. I may, when I get things untangled here, go in with somebody else. For the time being, we'll go on pretty much as before — except for Mary. Possibly Cuyler."

"Cuyler?"

"Frank's a good lawyer. He's a nice boy. But this isn't the kind of practice for him.

You've seen him — dramatic sort of man. Ideal trial lawyer. Push that hair of his back in front of a jury, turn on that intensity — phew! When we get into court at all, and we do our damnedest not to, it's usually before a judge who doesn't give a rap about intensity. Or hair, for that matter. Just wants precedents."

"Had this come up before?"

"Well — Forbes and I had talked about it."

"With Cuyler?"

"I hadn't. After all, Forbes was senior. That would have been his problem."

"And Karn?"

"Old Sol?" He smiled. "We mostly call him that. Not to his face, but he probably knows it. Probably amuses him, as much as he gets amused. As long as I stay in this kind of practice, I'll try to persuade Saul Karn to stick around. Knows more about copyright law than any man I know. More than I do. More than Forbes did, which says a lot. He and Sam Schaeffer — between them, they knew the works." He paused. "You're looking for motives in all this, of course?"

"For what I can find," Bill told him. "You realize that, counsellor."

"Poor old Mary, because she was going to be retired? Cuyler, because Forbes might have told him he'd be happier with another connection? Not very — persuasive, are they?"

"We have to take what we can get," Bill told him. "There's no scale for the weight of motives. Probably you know that. Something one person wouldn't notice might make someone else kill. We get murders for a five-dollar bill. Because a woman won't go back to a husband she doesn't like. One man says, 'All right, the hell with it.' Another man —" He ended with a shrug.

"Very well," Webb said. "I'll give you another — without prejudice, a better. Since you'll find out, anyway. I stand to gain a hundred thousand dollars from Forbes's death."

Bill Weigand raised eyebrows. Webb seemed pleased by the reaction. He nodded his head several times. He explained.

Each of the partners in the firm had carried insurance in favor of the others. The premiums had been paid by the firm, as such, but in effect each insured the others. In each case, the policy was for a hundred thousand dollars. In each case, the two surviving partners were beneficiaries, share and share alike. If only one survived, the money went to him.

"It's not uncommon, in any partnership," Webb said. "Some of our clients were, in effect, personal. Schaeffer had some; Ingraham brought some in. So did I. When Sam died,

93

some of his people went elsewhere. Some of Forbes will — say these friends of yours, the Norths. I barely knew North; we were attorneys for his publishing house because he knew Forbes and trusted him. Will he stay on? I don't know. So —"

So the insurance was to indemnify the surviving partners for the losses likely to be sustained. When Schaeffer had died, the insurance had been paid equally to Forbes Ingraham and to Webb. Ingraham's insurance would go to Webb.

"And Mrs. Schaeffer?"

"Not involved," Webb said. "This was strictly a matter of the partnership. Sam carried his own insurance and I suppose that went to Nan. I know it did, as a matter of fact. Sam was pretty well fixed anyway. So — Sam dies, and I get fifty thousand. Forbes dies, and I get another hundred. Of course, Sam wasn't murdered. Had an accident. But Forbes —"

"By the way," Bill Weigand said, "I gather there wasn't a double indemnity provision in Mr. Schaeffer's policy? Since you speak of getting fifty thousand."

"No," Webb said. "Turns out to have been an oversight, doesn't it? But — no. Not in this one." He waited a moment. "You wanted motives," he said. "You want a denial?"

94

"All right," Bill said. "Go ahead, Mr. Webb."

"I didn't kill Forbes."

"Theories?"

"You've thought of Halpern? And, if Forbes was right, the racketeers who were after Halpern? Might have decided to get Forbes. As they apparently tried to get Halpern himself."

"Right," Bill said. "I've thought of them, counsellor."

"Coming in through Sam's office and —"

Someone knocked on the office door. Bill Weigand said, "Come in, sergeant." Sergeant Mullins came in.

Mullins said, "This. In his desk."

He held "this" out. It was a key to a Yale lock. It was like any other key, except that it was made of gold.

Bill Weigand looked at it. He put it down on Reginald Webb's desk. It glowed there in the light from the desk lamp.

"Thought you'd want to see it, captain," Mullins said. "Who'd want a gold key?"

Weigand looked at Webb, and Webb nodded his head.

"Sam's," he said. "Sam's golden key. In whose desk, sergeant?"

Mullins looked at Bill Weigand, who nodded.

"Ingraham's," Mullins said. "Top center."

That, Webb told them, was rather odd. They waited.

"It's Sam Schaeffer's key to his office," Webb said. "What was his office — the key to the door from the outside corridor. I don't know why Forbes had it. I thought Mary put them somewhere after Sam died. All the office keys, I mean."

Schaeffer had had various keys to office locks — to the front door and to the door out of his office; to filing cases and other cabinets which were kept locked. A few of these were Schaeffer's only, opening personal files. The rest were duplicates of keys carried also by the other partners. They also had, for example, keys to the door which opened from Schaeffer's office to the public corridor. After his personal files had been cleared, and his personal possessions given to his wife, the office keys had been returned to the office, and given Mary Burton for safekeeping.

"Why this one turns up in Forbes's desk, I don't know," Webb said. "You'll want to talk to Mary?"

Weigand agreed they would want to talk to Mary. Webb used one of the telephones on his desk.

"Why gold?" Bill Weigand asked him, and at that Webb smiled. He said it had been Nan

96

Schaeffer's idea — a joke, and in a way not a joke.

"Sam was a great man for losing things," he said. "Misplacing them, rather. His ring of keys, his glasses, his wallet sometimes. He'd get down here without his keys and have to send the boy up before he could get his personal files open. So — Nan had one of the keys copied, and done in gold — gold filled, anyway. She said even Sam wouldn't leave a gold key lying around, and if he had it, he'd have them all."

"Did it work?"

"Matter of fact, I guess it did. Anyway, he wasn't always having to send Eddie over to the apartment. Not that the key's valuable in itself, particularly. But it apparently made him conscious of his keys. Kept on forgetting his glasses, but he kept extra pairs here. And — come in, Mary."

Mary Burton came in. She looked very tired; there was the vagueness of the weary in her movements. Bill said he was sorry they had had to keep her so late; she said, "Oh, it doesn't matter. Anything —"

"This key of Mr. Schaeffer's," Bill said, and held it toward her. "It's turned up in Mr. Ingraham's desk. Probably doesn't mean anything but still —"

"I don't know how it got there," she said.

She reached out for it. "When Mrs. Schaeffer gave them to me — all Mr. Schaeffer's keys, after he died — I put them in a file. One of the locked files, Mr. Webb. Under O, of course."

"O?"

"For office. They haven't been taken out since. At least —" She looked at the key. "I suppose Mr. Ingraham must have wanted it for something, although he had his own. I'll put it back with the others."

But Bill Weigand put out his hand for the little golden key, said he'd hold on to it for the time being. Mrs. Burton looked at Webb with doubt. "Of course, captain," Webb said. "Whatever you want." Bill took the key.

"This was with the other keys? When you put them in the file?"

"Oh yes," she said. "They were all on the chain. I put them in an envelope marked 'Mr. Schaeffer's office keys.' The chain, just as Mrs. Schaeffer gave it to me. Mr. Ingraham must have wanted it for something and —"

"Right," Bill said. He asked Webb for an envelope, got it, put the key in it and the envelope in a pocket. Then he stood up. It was a little after seven. He had, he told Reginald Webb, nothing more to ask them for the time being. He was sorry to have kept them so long. He said, "Come on, sergeant," and Mullins went on. They walked down Forty-fourth Street. Opposite the Algonquin, Bill suggested they might as well eat. They went in. At a table in the Oak Room they ordered drinks.

"You figure Ingraham loaned this key to somebody?" Mullins asked.

"Looks like it."

"So this somebody could come in and kill him without bothering anybody?"

"I doubt," Bill said gravely, "that that was in Ingraham's mind, Mullins. It may have worked out that way."

"Somebody he wanted to see without other people knowing," Mullins said, and sipped his old fashioned. "Don't put much sugar in 'em," he remarked. "A dame, most likely."

"Or," Bill said, "a client who didn't want to be seen."

"Why not just let them in?" Mullins asked. "I mean, this giving a key to somebody so's he can come in any time."

"I don't know, Mullins," Bill said. "Perhaps, as you say, it was a dame. Any particular dame in mind?"

"You notice that blond girl?" Mullins said. "Moore. Phyllis Moore? She was knocked by it — by Ingraham's being killed. For a girl who just worked there, she took it pretty hard. Could be, she worked overtime."

It could be, Bill agreed.

"He calls it off," Mullins said, and spiked out the cherry from his glass. "She takes it hard and shoots him. Then the key's no good any more, so she puts it in the desk and —" He stopped.

"Yes," Bill said. "There's a catch there, isn't there. You said the middle drawer? When he fell across the desk, his body pushed the drawer closed, if it was open. Held it closed, whether it was open before or not. So — the key was there before he was killed."

"O.K.," Mullins said. "She gave it back. He put it in the drawer. Then she shot him."

"It's not as good that way, is it?"

"Well," Mullins said, "pretty near. Of course — look who's here, Loot — I mean captain."

Pam and Jerry North were following Raul into the Oak Room. Pam waved. When they were nearer, she told Bill that they had been looking all over for him. Jerry looked at her. "Well," she said, "we were going to, right after dinner."

V

The police cannot be everywhere, and do not try to be. It was obvious that any of the seven men and women, counting a boy as a man, who worked in the law offices of Schaeffer, Ingraham and Webb might be the murderer of Ingraham. It was further obvious that if one of them was, any other who guessed at his identity might be in danger. In a city with enough policemen in it (but such a city does not exist anywhere) each of the seven might have been assigned to a pair of detectives — although three would really have been better — and so observed and, if need arose, protected. This would have required fourteen detectives, or twenty-one, and these were not available for so nebulous an enterprise.

So there was no official observation of Phyllis Moore, as, on the sidewalk in front of the office building in Forty-fourth Street, she said good night to Mary Burton and Dorothy

101

Lynch and began to walk east in Forty-fourth toward the Grand Central. She was slim and moved quickly; a cloth coat was wrapped tight about her and the wind hurried her along the sidewalk. When a tall man behind her, bareheaded in the cold air, said, "Wait a minute," she did not slow down her pace or look around. "What's the sense of this?" the man said, and overtook her without effort, and walked beside her.

"Leave me alone," Phyllis told Francis Cuyler. "Can't you leave me alone?"

"What's got into you?" he said, and kept pace. She did not say anything, but walked faster.

"All right," he said. "Ingraham's dead. I'm sorry. You're — all right, it's hit you hard. Because you thought — whatever you thought. I understand that."

"Leave me alone," she said. "Just leave me alone. Let me go."

"Not until I find out what you're thinking," he said. "You've got some idiotic idea in your head. You've been looking at me — when you thought I didn't see — as if —"

They were at the Fifth Avenue corner. Traffic stopped them. But then, without waiting for the lights to change, she ran into the traffic, stopped, started again, as cars swerved around her; as a bus slowed joltingly. She

102

reached the center of the street, but there the uptown traffic was too much for her — too much for the most darting flight. She stood, making herself narrow on the line which divided traffic.

She was alone for seconds only. Then Cuyler was beside her; and a hand on her arm. "You're crazy," he said. "You'll get yourself killed."

"Just leave me alone," she said.

The lights changed, the way opened. They were on the sidewalk, but he still held her arm. She did not, now, try to release herself.

"You've done enough," she said. "Haven't you done enough?"

"I don't know what you're talking about," he said. "If you've got something to say, say it."

She started on. He released her arm, but continued to walk beside her.

"Look," he said. "We'll have a cup of coffee. A drink, if you'd rather. We can't leave it this way."

She shook her head.

"I suppose," he said, and his voice was bitter. "I suppose you think I'd put poison in your drink? Or — what?"

She said nothing.

"All right," he said. "What do you think I've done — done that was 'enough'? Why don't you say it? Haven't you got the guts to say it?"

"You killed him," she said.

"All right. You've said it. You want to hear what I say?"

"What difference does it make? Oh — say it. Somebody'll believe you."

"I —" he said, and stopped, and swore. "We can't talk this way."

"There's nothing to talk about. I won't tell anybody. I couldn't prove anything, if I did."

"Here," he said, and took her arm again. He turned her toward the door of a restaurant. "We'll have a drink."

She did not resist, now; resistance seemed to have drained out of her. There was a cocktail area just inside the door. It was almost empty. He guided her to a table in a corner. A waiter came. "What do you want?" Cuyler said, and she said, "Oh, anything." "Martinis, then," he told the waiter. They came quickly; they were not particularly good. She left her glass standing before her, untouched.

"Why?" he said. "I suppose because I was jealous?"

"You hated him. Yesterday you said so. All but said so."

"He was all right. I was trying —" He shrugged. "I didn't hate him." He drank. "I guess it's no use," he said. "Don't know why

I thought it would be."

"I told you it was no use."

"When you don't want to believe things, you don't believe them. I thought I could — get to you. Get this crazy idea out of your head."

"You hated him. Oh — because of me. So, I can't say anything, can I? Because it was because of me. I can't be the one. You don't need to worry about what I'll say. If — if they find out, it won't be because of me."

"Oh, that," he said. His tone dismissed it. "It's what's between us —"

"Nothing. There's nothing between us."

"That's not true. You don't even think it's true."

She did not reply to that. She seemed merely to wait. He leaned toward her; he examined her face as if he had not seen it before. Her face did not change; she did not avoid his eyes, did not respond to them.

"All right," he said, finally. "You're a very pretty girl. You could be a very sweet girl. I'm in love with you, which is no secret. But, you're not very bright, are you?"

Her expression did not change.

"I didn't ask you," she said. "I asked you to leave me alone."

"No," he said. "Not very bright. That ought to make a difference. Well —"

"I'm going," she said. "You got what you wanted. Made me say what you knew I'd say. I don't know why you went to the trouble."

"No. I suppose you don't." He stood up. He looked at her untouched glass. "By God," he said, "you didn't really think — or is it bad form to drink with a murderer? Is that what the books say?"

She walked around the table toward the door. He made no move to follow her; said nothing further. After she had gone, he beckoned to the waiter. He ordered another martini. The waiter looked at the untouched glass.

"Lady didn't like it?" he said.

"No," Francis Cuyler said. "Didn't seem to, did she?"

There was no official observation of Mary Burton and Dorothy Lynch as, parting from Phyllis in front of the office building, they walked west in Forty-fourth Street — crossed The Avenue of the Americas, still universally thought of as Sixth Avenue, and went on to the subway station at Times Square. They parted there. Mrs. Lynch took an uptown express; Mrs. Burton a downtown train for South Ferry. They had said little as they walked; although side by side, each walked alone. Dorothy Lynch was hoping that her husband, already apprised of the cause of her lateness, would not take it into his well-meaning head to demonstrate that he was as good in the kitchen as the next man. She was simply too tired, too drained out, to face the kitchen after he had been good in it or, indeed, the more immediate product of his labors. What she wanted — what she needed — was to go out, to go to a restaurant, have a couple of drinks and a steak as far as possible from home cooked. She, in short, hoped to God that Ralph would not have taken it into his head to be considerate. Much as I love him, I suppose, Dorothy said to herself, and hung to a strap, swaying as the train swayed . . .

Mrs. Burton, having been widowed for a quarter of a century, had no such preoccupations. She did not think of food, or at any rate not of her own. She would, without doubt, just miss a ferry. One always just missed a ferry. She would have a sandwich and a cup of coffee, which would do very well. Poor Tommy — Mrs. Burton was not ingenious in the naming of cats — would merely have to wait. Well, he was too fat, anyway. They got that way when —

But she did not really think of these matters in any coherent manner. It is true that the predicament of Tommy briefly crossed the surface of her mind, as the shadow of a blown leaf may cross a murky pool. Mrs. Burton's consciousness remained submerged in muddled thought, and troubled by it. She had somehow mixed things up again. She knew this, was unhappily convinced of it, but she could not make herself remember what things she might have mixed up. This worried her.

It was frightening, it was really dreadful, to feel that her mind was not what it had once been. Twenty years ago — even five years ago — she had not forgotten things. She would not, then, conceivably have told Mr. Ingraham the Pierre when she meant the Roosevelt. "You're my memory, Mary," Sam Schaeffer had said often, in other years. "Couldn't get along without that head of yours," Forbes Ingraham had told her.

She did not deny that she was getting older, but she was not really old. A little over fifty — well, at any rate, somewhat under sixty. There was no reason why things should get mixed up; why she should forget things, and get them wrong. Only the little things, of course, but they could be so disconcerting. It was like trying to move through heavy mist. The outlines of things were blurred, wavering.

Now, since this terrible thing had happened, this unbelievable thing, she could hardly make herself think at all. If it was like being in a fog, it was also a little like trying to wake herself from a nightmare, as one may, knowing that what seems reality is only a dream, and hateful, but is still a tangle of fantasy against which struggle for a long time is futile. I must wake up; I must remember what I said wrong, Mary Burton thought, and walked through the ferry building toward the boat.

A boat had just come in, and she stood waiting — moving in an accustomed pattern, but still fighting against a dream — while, segregated in their own passageway, as if in a cattle chute, those the boat had released hurried onto the island of Manhattan. It was, she thought vaguely, an odd time to be going that way — away from home. Manhattan was for the daytime, for office time. In the evenings, one went the other way.

The gate opened and those who were waiting — not at this hour many, as many are reckoned in New York — began to cross the ramp onto the boat. Although there was no hurry, since the boat would wait, they hurried, jostling one another. Mary Burton went with them, onto the boat. But she went uneasily, almost reluctantly, still feeling dimly — and still striving to dispel the dimness — that she was leaving behind something undone, or done wrongly. She felt as she often felt on leaving her small house in the mornings, that she had forgotten something — that she had left water running somewhere or, perhaps, a lamp burning where Tommy might knock it over and start a fire. (That had almost happened once. He — it could only have been Tommy — had upset a lamp with a silk shade, and it had fallen so that the hot bulb, unbroken, was pressed against the fabric. Fire had not actually started, but the shade had been charred deeply.) It was like that now — water left running, a light burning, a door unlocked.

She stood just on the boat, not entering the cabin. A deck hand had reached for the folding gate when she remembered. She said, "Oh. Wait," and almost ran off the ferryboat. The deck hand looked at her, and shrugged his shoulders, and closed the gate.

She was not sure even now, again in the ferry waiting room. She was sure only of what she was not sure, and in what her uncertainty lay. And, so remembered or partially remembered, the thing which had bothered her seemed of greatly diminished importance. It was a relief to have put her mind on it; encouraging to discover that, when she really tried, she could remember as well as ever. But the whole matter was not, probably, worth having missed a boat over. However —

She found a telephone booth, and dialed a number, by no means needing to find it in the directory. She listened to the sound which meant that the telephone she had dialed was ringing; waited long enough to know that it was to remain unanswered. Well, she had not really expected anything else.

She replaced the receiver and hesitated. Then she consulted the Manhattan directory and this time she dialed a number unfamiliar to her, but familiar enough — Spring 7-3100. It was not the best number she could have selected for her purpose, but it was good enough, and this time she was very promptly answered.

"The officer in charge of the investigation of Mr. Ingraham's death," she said. "I think he was a captain — a Captain Weigand, isn't it?"

It was. She waited, while at a telephone switchboard a man's fingers worked briskly. Again she was quickly answered: "Homicide West. Stein."

She asked for Captain Weigand; was told that he was not in, was asked if anyone else would do. She hesitated.

"No," she said. "I think —"

"A message?" Sergeant Stein asked.

"If you'd tell him that Missis —" she began, and stopped. "No," she said. "I'll call him tomorrow. Thank you."

She replaced the receiver once more, and opened the door of the telephone booth and started out. But she stopped again, and hurried back, and dialed another number.

It took somewhat longer this time, but she was answered.

"This is Mary Burton," she said. "I hope I'm not interrupting anything?"

"No."

"About this dreadful thing. Poor Mr. Ingraham."

"Yes."

"I was on my way home and I got to worrying. I thought I remembered and then I wasn't sure and I wondered if you remembered. About —"

She told of the little worrying thing. She listened, then. She began to nod toward the mouthpiece, as if toward the person to whom she listened.

"Of course," she said, and then, "I'm so glad you do. I was so afraid I'd —"

She listened again, momentarily. She said, again, "I do hope I didn't interrupt anything."

She hung the receiver up and this time left the booth. She went to a lunch counter and ate a baked Virginia ham sandwich, which was neither baked nor from Virginia. She drank coffee.

It would be untrue to say that, when Mary Burton boarded the next ferry, her mind was at ease. But it was free to worry about other things — more important things. There would be changes in the firm — more than there had been when Mr. Schaeffer had died. There was only Mr. Webb now. It was hard to tell what would happen.

Reginald Webb left the law offices some little time after the departure of Cuyler, and the three women, and Eddie, but he was not the last to leave. There was a light in the library, and Webb looked into it. Saul Karn sat at one end of the long table, under the light. He was surrounded, seemed to be walled behind, a number of reasonably ponderous volumes. He was engaged in inserting slips of paper between pages and this was, indeed, one of the major occupations of his life. At the appearance of Webb, Karn inserted a slip — at "The People of the State of New York vs John Doe, et al" — took his glasses off, and looked up.

"Still at it?" Webb said.

Since he so evidently was, Karn regarded the question as both rhetorical and ridiculous, and was briefly tempted to say, "What's it look like?" in reply. But what he said, without emphasis, was "Yes."

"What do you think?" Webb said. "They getting anywhere?"

"Probably," Karn said. "They usually do, sooner or later."

"Not always."

"No."

Karn put fingers at his marked place, preliminary to reopening the volume, since he saw little point in continuing an exchange of the obvious. Webb was unduly given to conversation. Most people were unduly given to something, and Saul Karn had long accepted this fact, without prejudice. Even Forbes Ingraham, a considerably better lawyer than Webb, had been unduly given to matters obviously extraneous — matters only to be described as emotional. This last matter, for example, had been quixotic. In a manner of speaking, Ingraham had only himself to blame.

"Want to get on with it, don't you, Saul?" Webb said, and his voice was tolerant. Karn, who had replaced his rimless glasses on his nose, again removed them.

"Yes," he said.

"See to things before you go, then?" Webb said.

"Certainly," Karn said, extending himself. He resumed his glasses and opened the book in which he was seeking a suitable precedent.

"Good night," Webb said. To this, Karn merely nodded his head. Webb looked at him for a moment, and shook his. Then Webb left.

114

By the time he was in the elevator, Reginald Webb had forgotten Saul Karn, having other things to think about. Unlike Mrs. Burton, he knew precisely what worried him. This did not make matters any better.

Left to himself, Saul Karn continued through the appropriate pages of several more volumes, putting marking slips where they would do the most good. With that, he had traced a precedent to what was almost certainly its lair. He put the volumes concerned in a neat pile and returned the remaining volumes to the shelves. With that done, Saul Karn proceeded to other matters.

He proceeded to the office safe, and opened it. He took a locked deed box from the safe and opened it. From the box, he removed a sheaf of legal sized yellow paper. He was gratified to discover that the sheaf was still where, on instructions, he had placed it.

He did not return yellow sheets to the deed box, but put them instead in his brief case. It had been suggested that he keep this to himself, for the time being. Circumstances being what they now were, this instruction could not indefinitely be followed. Nor was there any precise precedent. The next step needed to be thought over until an appropriate conclusion was reached. Karn had no doubt whatever of his ability to reach the conclusion which, under the given circumstances, would be proper.

He went through Ingraham's office then, and through the one beyond it which had been occupied by Sam, and there, in an office so evidently long unused, Saul Karn shook his head sadly and thought, "poor old Sam," letting the disorder of remembrance creep for a moment into his orderly mind. He then dismissed these intruding thoughts, and made sure that the door from the office to the outside corridor was securely locked. He found it was, and thought, "for what that's worth," noting, as he had noted before, that the heavy old door no longer fitted snugly in the jamb. To a man with a screw driver and a moderate amount of experience it would not, Karn was sure, matter whether the door was locked or not. Probably the whole jamb was little more than coherent sawdust.

There was nothing to do about that, except what he had already done. Saul Karn went out of the offices, carrying his brief case, turning off lights behind him, making sure that the front door also was locked. He waited some time for the elevator, which was no longer on rush hour schedule, and said a brief good night to the operator, no longer in uniform, who took him down. In Forty-fourth Street, he walked briskly eastward toward Grand

Central and he, also, was not officially observed. He passed, without noticing, a parked sedan in which three men were sitting in conversation.

For some fifteen minutes, Reginald Webb had been sitting between two men, neither of whom he had before met, in the back seat of a parked car. A third man, also not of Webb's acquaintance, sat behind the wheel, and did not turn his head.

It was dark in the car, and the men who sat on either side of Webb had snap brim hats pulled rather low. The man on Webb's left, canted his hat to the right; the man on the other side preferred a leftward cant. When Webb had started to light a cigarette, the man on his left, who was the more loquacious of the two, had requested him not to. He had said it was bad for his laryngitis. At this, the other man, who previously had said only, "Fella would like to see you, Mr. Webb," said, "Yeah, and light hurts my eyes."

"Don't try to be funny," the other man said. "At being funny, you're no good."

The man who was no good at being funny had made his other remark when Webb, coming from the office building, had hesitated near the curb, hoping for a cab. The man had come up beside Webb and said that a fella would like to see him, and had said it, out of a small tight mouth, in the voice of a man who has a gun in his coat pocket. There was no real evidence of this, although the man did keep his right hand in a pocket. Webb had walked with the man for perhaps fifty feet to a parked car, and the man had taken his hand from his pocket and opened the door. The man already sitting inside had said, "Good evening, Mr. Webb. Won't keep you a minute." Webb had not got a good view of the man then, or since.

"Sorry to hear about Ingraham," the man had said. "That was tough luck." He paused. "For him," he added.

"Very," Webb said. He was not particularly frightened, although he would have preferred to be elsewhere. "What's the idea?" he said, then.

"Too bad about your partner," the fella who had wanted to see Webb said. "Shows a man's got to be careful, don't it?" He paused a moment. "Don't it, Mr. Webb?"

"I don't know what it shows," Webb said. "What's the idea of this?"

"People get careless," the man said. "Even lawyers — they get careless like anybody else. Pick the wrong clients, things like that. Did you ever think of that, counsellor?"

"If you've got a point —" Webb said. He

moved forward in his seat. The man who had first accosted him moved forward also, moving closer to Webb.

"Don't bump the counsellor," the other man said. "Everything nice and friendly. The point is Halpern, counsellor. Matt Halpern? You've heard of Matt?"

"Obviously," Webb said. "He's a client. The client you mean?"

"Ingraham's client," the man said. "Hear Ingraham more or less went after him. Thought that wasn't ethical, counsellor. What they call a shyster trick."

"Get to the point," Webb said. "I've got an engagement."

"Now you," the man said. "I'd figure you're ethical, Mr. Webb. High class type lawyer. Wouldn't want to get mixed up in anything. See what I mean?"

"Well," Webb said. "Thanks. Have you got a name?"

"That's what I mean," the talkative man said, across Webb, to the other. "Mr. Webb knows how to be funny. Sure I've got a name, counsellor. Ever know a man without a name? Getting back to Matt Halpern. Not the right type client for an ethical man like you, counsellor. Careful man. Not a careless man. Like Mr. Ingraham turned out to be."

"Suppose you come to the point?"

"That's right. You got a date. Keep forgetting that. All right, counsellor — let Matt Halpern find another lawyer. See what I mean? Ingraham's dead. Way I figure, you might keep Halpern on. Use any — well, say any dope Ingraham might have got together. That would be sort of careless of you, Mr. Webb."

"Who represents him is up to Mr. Halpern," Webb said.

"Is that right?" the man said. "You know what I'd think? I'd think Mr. Ingraham dying that way would sort of mess things up in an office. For awhile, anyway. Maybe have more clients than you could handle. See what I mean?"

"Halpern would merely get another lawyer," Webb said. "Better one, maybe, for what he wants. Somebody in criminal practice."

"Sure," the man said. "That's what I call ethical, Mr. Webb. Gets himself another lawyer. Starts fresh. Better for everybody. Shouldn't wonder if Halpern hasn't already thought of that. Maybe thought of the man he wants."

"Look," Webb said, "are you supposed to be speaking for Halpern? You expect me to believe that?"

"Just for myself," the man said. "Matt

speaks for himself. I speak for myself."

"And tell me to lay off Halpern. Threaten me if I don't."

"Threatening you? Don't know what you mean by that. Know what he means by that?"

"No," the other man said. "Nobody's pushed him around."

"Like he says," the talkative man said. "No pushing around. Just don't like to see a man get careless — ethical type man like you. That's all it is."

"It's up to Halpern."

"Tell you," the man said. "You think about it, counsellor. Just think about it, counsellor. That's friendly advice. Get out of Mr. Webb's way, huh? He's got an engagement, like he said."

The man on Webb's right opened the car door, and got out of it. He held it open for Webb. Webb got out. "Nice talking to you," the man who had remained in the back seat said. The other man got back in the car. Webb began to walk away, and felt his back muscles tightening. But nothing happened.

It was a few minutes after eight when Reginald Webb walked past the statuary in the front yard of "21" and through the door opened for him. He checked his hat and coat and responded to several "Good evening, Mr. Webb" greetings, and was aware that he was

121

looked at with more than usual interest — with a kind of sympathy, held in reserve if asked for. He did not ask for it. He went into the lounge, where Milton Berle was just beginning to convulse on the television screen. It appeared that, although late, Webb was earlier than she was. He sat on a sofa and looked absently at the screen, and was not convulsed. After a time he ordered a drink.

It was almost eight-thirty when Nan Schaeffer came into the lounge. She wore a dark silk suit under her mink coat. She came around the sofa in front of him, and he stood up.

"I'm sorry, Reg," she said. "I got held up. Have you been waiting a long time?"

"It's all right," he said and then, looking at her, "You all right, Nan?"

"I know," she said. "I don't look it. Yes, I'm all right. I won't say I feel like dancing in the streets. Do you?"

"No," he said. "You want a drink here?"

She did not, if a table was ready. A table was, and they went up the wide stairs to it. She moved, he thought, as if she were tired; sitting beside her at the table, he noticed again the pallor of her face, and the strain in it. She pulled the mink coat over her shoulders as if, in the warm restaurant, she still were cold.

"I was talking to Mr. and Mrs. North," she

said. "Phoebe wanted to — wanted me to. She's taking it very hard, Reg. It doesn't show, but she is. Or — I guess it does show."

"It's tough on her," he said. "Tough on everybody. Why the Norths?"

"She thinks the police won't try. If it's all mixed up with a racket. She thinks the Norths might help. I don't see how they can, do you?"

He said he didn't.

"Would the police try to cover up for people like that? Racketeers?"

"I don't know," Webb said. "I doubt it. Not murder. Not murder of a man like Forbes."

"They might try to make it seem it was somebody else? To protect these people?"

"I don't know. Why did Phoebe want you to talk to the Norths?"

"Because of something Forbes said yesterday. And the way he acted."

She told him what she had told Pam and Jerry North.

He nodded his head when she had finished. He said it fitted.

"I ran into a couple of men after I left the office," he said. "They tried to scare me off."

He told her the rest of it. When he had told it, she leaned toward him and put a hand briefly on one of his. She was less pale, then; there was less weariness in her face. But she

123

said, "Darling. I'm afraid. Will you do what they want?"

"Not unless Halpern wants it that way. Maybe he will." He paused and drank. "I'm not saying I want to be mixed up in it."

"Have you told the police?"

"Not yet."

"Reg! You must."

"Oh, I'll tell them. But I can't describe the men, except that one of them — the one who took me to the car — had a small mouth. I can't say they threatened me. They didn't, directly. And — it will sound pretty pat, Nan."

She shook her head, raised her eyebrows in question.

"They look for the one who profits," he told her. "I do."

"No," she said. "Oh *no!* They couldn't think that."

He said he hoped not.

"It's so obvious," she said. "The way Forbes acted. Almost as if he expected something — something like what happened. And then these men threatening you. What else could it be?"

The waiter captain waited, expectant, detached. They ordered.

"You remember Sam's gold key," he said, as a statement, and to the statement she nodded her head. "It's turned up," he said, and told her where. She shook her head to that.

"You sent it back, didn't you?"

"Of course. With the others."

"For some reason," he said, "Forbes seems to have taken it. I suppose to give it to someone. So whoever it was could go into his office without being seen. And — then took it back. Just before he was killed, probably."

He looked at her and waited.

"Phoebe," she said. "It would almost have to be Phoebe, wouldn't it?"

"It's an idea," he agreed. "Only —"

But a waiter brought them fresh drinks, then, and, very promptly, another brought oysters, which are so admirable with martinis which are very dry and very, very cold.

Dr. Aaron Arn sat in a deep chair and sipped scotch and plain water, since alcohol should be drunk in dilute form and charged water irritates the digestive tract, which Dr. Arn thought of more simply as the gut. Gin, which all reasonable people prefer before meals, merges discontentedly with tap water. He smoked a cigarette, which he presumed would eventually lead to cancer of the lung, and read an evening newspaper which, if taken seriously, would inevitably lead to psychic trauma. Dr. Arn did not pay particular attention to what he read.

This slow sipping of a diluted drink, this half-attentive consideration of the evening paper, this inhalation of smoke which might (but on the other hand might not; people jumped wildly to conclusions) damage his lungs, was a ritual of relaxation. Some minutes before he had, finally, seen his last patient of the day. He had walked from the office through a corridor and into the apartment. Mrs. Arn had had the drink ready and the paper neatly to hand, and she had said, "Tired, dear?"

"A little," he said, and sat down, and Mrs. Arn withdrew, on the unspoken pretext that she must see how dinner was coming. In half an hour he would join her, and this time they would have a drink together, and talk. It was pleasant that they still had so much to say, after so long a time. But this interval was prescribed; now Dr. Aaron Arn merely sat, and pretended to read.

There was a headline across the first page, beyond which Dr. Arn had not got. It read: "Lawyer Found Slain at Desk." Dr. Arn read this, since it was inescapable. It made little impression on him. In one fashion or another, all men died. All hearts stopped, on one pretext or another, however one sought to keep them beating. This was obvious, although un-

126

derstandably difficult to explain to patients.

Nevertheless, for want of other interest — in a kind of inertia — Dr. Arn read further in the inverted pyramids of type which were below the headline. He came upon a name and blinked at it. Forbes Ingraham. It was somewhat familiar. A patient? Dr. Arn considered. If so, a new one. He would have to ask Florence about it in the —

Dr. Arn blinked again, remembering. He put down the newspaper and remembered further. Not a patient. The man who —

It was only twenty-five minutes after he had sat down in the living room that Dr. Arn left it and joined his wife in the library. Mrs. Arn looked up in some surprise. Her husband was carrying *The World Telegram and Sun* with him, and her surprise was enhanced. It was not, ordinarily, allowed in the library.

"This man —" Dr. Arn said, and pointed at the headline. "This morning he —"

VI

Tuesday, 8:50 P.M. to Wednesday, 12:30 A.M.

For those who go two by two, in proper fashion, the Algonquin's Oak Room is a restaurant of many charms, and provides such isolation as is appropriate, and all that is generally desired. Parties of four are less secluded; such confidential matters as murder are less conveniently discussed. After dinner, therefore, the Norths, Weigand and Mullins, went to the Norths' apartment to exchange notes on progress. They were greeted by the cats, who were disappointed to find them so many, and audible in disapproval. The Norths, in what amounted to responsive readings, told of their tea with Phoebe James and Nan Schaeffer.

"Is she a good author, Jerry?" Pam said, of Mrs. James, and Jerry said she sold extremely well, was told not to avoid the issue.

"Because," Pam said, "she seems apologetic about what she does."

Many writers were, or allowed that inference to be drawn, Jerry told her. Mrs. James was good; on occasion she was very good. She wrote for a large audience, and Jerry, morosely, wished more did. Some years before a writer of magazine fiction, she had more recently been writing historical novels — "and very good ones." Her plots were particularly expert.

"Hm-m," said Pam North, with meaning. Jerry and Bill Weigand looked at each other; they shared their look with Mullins. They shook heads.

"Hm-m what?" Jerry said.

"Just hm-m. Of course, it could all be, because otherwise it's a little thin. Anybody can see that."

"No," Jerry said, as spokesman. "What is, Pam?"

"Having us there," Pam said. "Wanting us to help. Bringing poor Mrs. Schaeffer in."

"Why," Jerry said, carefully, "why 'poor' Mrs. Schaeffer?"

"Because her husband's dead, of course," Pam said. "You're not very perceptive, Jerry. And all this nonsense about the police protecting the ones who did it. I smell a red herring."

"You mean," Jerry began, and decided against continuing. Undoubtedly, red herrings were as olfactorily detectable as rats. "Is it nonsense, Bill? I don't mean as far as you're

129

concerned, of course."

"Do hoods get protection?" Bill said. "Yes, sometimes. Under some circumstances. From some men. You want a lecture on it? During prohibition — remember prohibition? — sure. Nobody wanted prohibition. Bookmaking — yes, some of the boys play ball. It's a ridiculous law. There are twenty thousand policemen in the department. Among twenty thousand men you can find any kind you're looking for — twenty thousand cops or business men or union men or bankers. If the commissioner found anybody covering up murder the man would never stop bouncing. End lecture."

"Why," Pam said, "would a woman like Mrs. James not realize that? Because she believes what she reads in the papers? Before elections?"

"Perhaps."

"I didn't think so," Pam said. "Anyway, I don't think gangsters — hoods. Because they kill themselves and Forbes wasn't one." She looked at the others. "Kill each other," she said, cleaning matters up.

Bill shook his head at that. Attorneys with racketeering clients had been killed before now. Giving Matthew Halpern the benefit of the doubt; assuming — as Forbes Ingraham evidently had — that Halpern opposed rackets rather than joined them, there remained some support for Mrs. James's theory. Particularly since what Mrs. Schaeffer said supported it, the attack on Halpern supported it, the evidently cautious meeting between Ingraham and Halpern at the restaurant supported it.

"Enough," he said, "for us to put a couple of men on Halpern. Which reminds me — mind calling in, sergeant?"

Mullins called in. He reported. Halpern had had dinner at a lunch counter. He had gone, unmolested, to his room in an inexpensive West Side hotel. He apparently remained there. Nothing else had developed.

"Oh yeah," Mullins said. "Somebody wanted you, Loot." He shook his head. "Captain," he said, with emphasis. "Woman. Didn't give her name. Started to and stopped. Missis somebody. She'll call back tomorrow."

"Right," Bill said. "Now, among the things that don't support the theory you don't like, Pam: Webb stands to gain a hundred thousand dollars from his partner's death. And somebody left a gold key."

He told them of the insurance arrangement, and of the keys. As he told of the latter, Pamela North began to nod her head.

"That," she said, as he finished, "explains everything, doesn't it?"

She waited for response with the air of one who expects it to be instantaneous. She did not receive it, and seemed surprised.

"I'd think you'd see how it all fits together," she said. "Forbes gave Mrs. James the key, of course. Who else would he give a *gold* key to? A regular key, to anybody. But to her, a gold key. As a symbol. But then he falls in love with this girl at the office — this —"

"Phyllis Moore," Bill told her.

"This Phyllis. Not the other way around, as Mrs. James said. And *that* was why she wanted us — not the gangster things from Mrs. Schaeffer. So she could plant it upside down."

"Wait," Jerry said.

"Not the girl in love with him, and he paternal about it. He with her — maybe both with each other. And Mrs. James finds out and —" She stopped. "Well?" she said. "Of course, it's a triangle, but it's better than gangsters. And poor Mrs. Schaeffer's just being used."

There was something in what she said, Bill agreed, and spoke slowly. When you got it untangled, Jerry North added, and he was looked at. What Pam called the symbolic nature of the gold key — that was a point. Of course, the key originally —

The telephone rang. Jerry answered it, handed the instrument to Bill Weigand. Bill listened, said "Right" twice, and made finger gestures for pencil and paper.

"Dr. Aaron Arn," he repeated, and repeated an address on Park Avenue, writing. He said, "Thanks, sergeant," and hung up.

"Ingraham made an appointment with a doctor," he said, and indicated the name he had written down. "For this afternoon. An appointment he couldn't keep, as it turned out."

They waited.

"Apparently," he said, "not as a patient. At least, the doctor got that impression. Ingraham seems to have been — well, a little cryptic."

They waited. They were told that that was all.

"What does it mean?" Jerry asked.

Bill Weigand said he hadn't the faintest idea. He said he thought he had better try to find out. He said, "Come on, Mullins," and they went.

"Well," Pam North said, "don't you agree about Mrs. James?"

Jerry hoped not. He hated, as a matter of general principle, to see anything happen to authors who sold well. Authors sometimes grew dissatisfied with publishers that they had, and flew to others that they knew not of.

"As," Pam said, "in the famous case of the

133

frying pan and the fire."

Dr. Aaron Arn was a man of sixty-odd, rather narrow-shouldered, gray-haired, and he looked at Captain William Weigand and Sergeant Aloysius Mullins through very alert gray eyes. Bill was fleetingly conscious, as one often is when observed by physicians, that his life expectancy was being shrewdly, if more or less instinctively, gauged. He resisted an impulse to say, "Well, doctor, how do I look?" He identified himself, instead.

Dr. Arn had received them in his office. He did not wear a white coat, nor have a stethoscope around his neck nor a mirror on his forehead. He said that, now he had thought it over, he feared he had brought them on a wild-goose chase. He said that his wife, however, had felt strongly that, although the significance of what he had to tell was by no means apparent, he should get in touch with the police about it. He placed considerable confidence in the judgment of his wife.

"I can't say," he told them across an uncluttered desk, "that I expected such a prompt response."

They tried, Weigand told him, to waste no more time than they had to. They tried to pick up everything. Much that they picked up did not appertain, and that was the lot of a policeman. "You must often examine patients and find nothing," Bill suggested.

"Now and then," Dr. Arn said. "But that, of course, is also something."

To a degree, it was the same with the police. So?

At about nine-thirty that morning, before Dr. Arn left the living area of his suite for the office, a telephone call had come through and been switched to him by his secretary. The caller identified himself as Forbes Ingraham, and asked for an appointment. Dr. Arn had said that he had regular office hours — from ten in the morning until noon, in the evening from five to seven. "Which usually means eight, sometimes nine," he added, with a moderate sigh.

That did not satisfy Forbes Ingraham. He wanted an appointment outside office hours; some time in mid-afternoon, if that was possible. And he did not want to see the doctor as a patient.

Dr. Arn had hesitated, then.

"Normally," he told Weigand and Mullins, "I would have told him that I did not make special appointments, except under very unusual circumstances, and then only with patients. Or personal friends, of course. Or for consultations. But there was something about this man. You knew him, captain?"

135

Bill shook his head.

"He spoke very softly," Dr. Arn said. "Without much emphasis — none of this I'm-an-important-man sort of business. No — what do they say? — no throwing his weight around. And yet you felt you were talking with somebody of importance. Do I make it clear at all? Importance is an absurd word, of course, but it does come to mind."

"He was a very able man," Bill told him. "Very widely known in his profession. You hadn't heard of him?"

Dr. Arn could not remember that he had, or had not remembered when he was talking to Ingraham.

"But perhaps, subconsciously, I did remember having heard his name."

In spite of this feeling, Dr. Arn had still hesitated.

"It is quite important, doctor," Ingraham had said then, in his soft, oddly compelling voice. "I'll need only a few minutes of your time."

"I asked him to give me some idea what it was all about," Dr. Arn said. "I asked him what all the mystery was. I felt there was some mystery, although I don't precisely know why. He said he would much rather not take it up on the telephone. The upshot was, I agreed to see him at three. Usually, that would be

136

impossible — I'm usually at the hospital during the afternoon. But I'd just got back from a conference and things are a little quiet. At the hospital, that is. Anyway — As you realize, of course, he didn't come. I was annoyed, naturally. Then I read —"

"He gave you no idea what he wanted?"

"None, captain. It's not very tangible, is it? Or, helpful, I'm afraid."

On the face of it, Bill agreed, it was difficult to see how it helped. But, one never knew. "Among other things," he said, "we are interested in anything out of the way. Any unexplained action, by anyone concerned."

"My wife thought you probably were," Dr. Arn said. "As symptomatic, in a sense."

"Right," Bill said. "By the way, you're a specialist, doctor?"

"I'm an internist," Dr. Arn said. "Say I specialize in general medicine. Diagnosis."

He looked at Weigand.

"I suppose that doesn't help, particularly," he said.

"No. You got no inkling at all of what he wanted? Can't guess?"

Arn shook his head.

"Except that he did not want to see me as a patient. Puzzling, isn't it? Of course, if it weren't in this — this context — still, I don't know. It would still be odd."

It was. Bill shook his head over it. Why would a man, not a patient or planning to become one, make an appointment with a physician to discuss something which he could not — Bill's thoughts focused.

"If I gave you some names, doctor, would you tell me whether they are patients? Just that, of course. I realize you couldn't go further."

"Under the circumstances," Dr. Arn said. "Yes."

"Then," Bill said, and named names — Reginald Webb? Mary Burton? Phyllis Moore? To each Arn, after a moment of thought, shook his head. "Francis Cuyler? Saul Karn?" Again the gray head was shaken in the negative. "Phoebe James?" Arn started again to shake his head. But then he said, "Wait." He opened a drawer of his desk, and checked on a card file. "Yes," he said. "About a year ago. She was here once. Is she —?" He did not finish.

"Ingraham and she were friends," Bill told him. "A man named Halpern? Matthew Halpern?"

"No."

Bill was running low. Who else?

"A Mrs. Schaeffer? Mrs. Samuel Schaeffer?"

"I don't think — yes, I believe she was in once. Sent over by —" He stopped. He looked at his file again.

"Yes," he said. "Once. And her husband too. He was —" He stopped. He snapped his fingers. "That's why I felt Ingraham's name was familiar," he said. "Schaeffer, Ingraham and Webb, the paper says. I must have put it together without realizing it."

"Probably," Bill said.

"But," Dr. Arn said, "is it anything that helps you? I can't, of course, tell you any more about patients. You realize that?"

"Oh yes," Bill said. "Since —"

"Since," Dr. Arn said, "Mrs. James and Mrs. Schaeffer are alive. And Mr. Schaeffer died accidentally. If he'd done as I —" He shrugged. "Well," he said, "I've given you all I can, captain. So —"

It was, politely, a suggestion of dismissal, by a man who had done his civic duty, and had had a long day. "Unless there's something else?"

There was not. Weigand and Mullins left the office, walked out into Park Avenue, and to their car.

"I don't see where it gets us," Mullins said. "What Ingraham died of, a doctor couldn't do anything about."

It was, Bill Weigand agreed, difficult for a physician to include gunshot wounds in his prognosis; would have been, even if Ingraham had been a patient. They would go back to West Twentieth Street, and see whether anybody else had got further.

" '— the big rock candy mountain,' " Pam North sang, moderately in unison with Burl Ives. " 'Oh, the buzzzzzzzing of the bees and the cigarette trees' — Mr. Ives can buzz longer than I can."

Mr. Ives, Jerry told her, could buzz longer than anyone.

"Except another bee," Pam said. " 'And the soda water fountain. Where the —' "

Martini had had enough. On Pam's lap she growled warningly; she turned, extended herself up Pamela, and put a dark brown paw firmly on Pam's parted lips.

"Well!" Pam said. "So that's the way you feel."

"Ruowruh," Martini said, not loudly but with conviction.

"Sometimes," Jerry said, "it occurs to me we rather spoil that cat."

Martini, without removing her paw from Pam's lips, turned her head and looked flatly at Jerry, from blue eyes. The tip of her tail twitched.

"That'll teach you," Pam said, around the paw. "I —"

The telephone rang; it was very sudden and

loud in the apartment. "Hell," Jerry said, and stood up, the other two cats pouring from where his lap had been. "At this time of night."

It was eleven-fifteen, which is not particularly a time of night, unless one is sheltered before a fire, with cats about, with Mr. Ives singing. (It was "Foggy, Foggy Dew" by now.) Jerry turned off the record player; he said, "Hello," with no enthusiasm in his tone.

"Mrs. North!" a woman's voice said. The voice was high-pitched, strained.

"Wait," Jerry said. "She's here. If —"

"Oh!" the woman said. *"Hurry — please hurry!"*

Pam was already beside Jerry. She took the telephone. She said, "Yes. Who is it?"

"Nan Schaeffer," the voice said. It seemed near hysteria. *"Oh — I was so afraid you wouldn't —"*

"What is it?" Pam said.

"You've got to help me," Nan Schaeffer said, and her voice, although it was not loud, had the texture of a scream. "I can't make the police under —"

There was a momentary pause, then. Pam held the telephone a little from her ear, and Jerry leaned closer.

"No!" Nan Schaeffer said, and now her voice did rise, now was a scream in Pam

141

North's ear. "Don't — I — *don't* — oh — *please* —"

And then the voice stopped. There was the silence — the strange, hollow silence — of an open telephone circuit.

"Mrs. Schaeffer!" Pam said. *"Mrs. Schaeffer!"*

There was only the hollow silence, for a second. Then a click filled the emptiness and the line was dead.

Pam called once more into the dead telephone, stood holding it, turned to Jerry.

"You heard?" she asked.

Jerry had heard. He ran a hand through his hair. "What the hell?" he asked, of nobody who had an answer.

Pam was dialing, by then. In the matter of seconds, she was answered. "Homicide, Stein." In seconds more, she had learned that Weigand had just left, calling it a night. Pam spoke rapidly, telling of the call; said, "I don't know, sergeant. I haven't any idea" when Stein asked whether there had been any indication as to where Nan Schaeffer had called from.

"She lives in a hotel," Pam said. "The —" She stopped. "I almost know," she said. "It was the —" But she stopped again, memory snagged. But surely Nan Schaeffer had named the hotel? "I can't remember," she told Sergeant Stein. "But — I don't think it came from a hotel. Not through a switchboard. Of course, Jerry answered first and — wait." The wait was momentary. "No," she said. "Not through a switchboard, he thinks too. What do we do, sergeant?"

"We'll pick up Bi — Captain Weigand," Stein said. "I don't know there's anything you can do, Mrs. North. We'll get on it."

He hung up.

The East Plaza! Pam said, memory freed. "The — He's hung up."

She dialed again, but this time the telephone rang unanswered. Only after almost a minute did a flat voice say, "Homicide, Flaherty."

"Pamela North," Pam said. "Sergeant Stein?"

"Not here. Got a call and went out to — who did you say this was?"

"North," Pam said. "Mrs. North."

"Huh?"

"Isn't there anybody?" Pam said, her voice desperate. "Sergeant Stein? Mullins?"

"Look, lady. Stein's gone out of the office, like I said. Mullins went home hours ago. What do you want, lady? Sergeant Stein's all tied up. If you want something —"

"The East Plaza," Pam said. "Will you tell the sergeant that? The East Plaza."

"East Plaza," Flaherty said. "That mean something, lady?"

"A hotel," Pam said. "It's — will you just tell him, Mr. Flaherty? *East Plaza. Mrs. Schaeffer.*"

"Have to ask you to spell that, lady," Detective Flaherty said. "I just came in."

"S —" Pam began, and stopped. "Please," she said. "Please. Just tell somebody. It's important and —"

"Sure, lady. Don't get excited. Soon as I see the sergeant I'll —"

But Pam North hung up, then.

"There's nobody there," she told Jerry. "He keeps calling me 'lady.' Come on."

Jerry started to ask, "Where?" but decided he knew. There was no stopping Pam, in any event. She fled along a corridor, seeking coat. "We're the ones she called," Pam said, her head in a closet, but the words none-the-less clear. "That man will never get it straight."

Taxicabs grow less numerous, except in the theater district, as midnight nears. It took the Norths time to find one in the windy street. But, once found, the cab went fast. It was a little after twelve when the cab swerved to the curb in front of a marquee lettered, discreetly, "The East Plaza" and the driver said, with triumph, "Here you are."

The clerk was immaculate. He was also talking on a telephone, with great charm, but little speed. Pam tapped nails on the counter, and he nodded and smiled over the telephone, and made lip movements of encouragement. Finally he finished.

"Mrs. Schaeffer," Jerry said. "Mrs. Samuel Schaeffer."

"Mrs. —" the clerk began, and stopped. He looked at them with a rather odd expression, which included narrowed eyes. "Mrs. Schaeffer," he said. "Yes. Twelve-oh-four."

"We can —" Pam began.

"Go right on up," the clerk said. "Yes."

They went, but agreed, on the way, that it was odd. "A very *funny* hotel," Pam said, and then went down a carpeted corridor. They rang a bell.

The door opened instantaneously, as if a hand had been ready on the inner knob.

"Oh," Bill Weigand said. He looked at them. "Well, now you're here," he said, and let them in. There was, Pam thought, disappointment in his voice, and surprise at this was reflected on her face. "Thought you might be somebody more felonious," Bill said, and grinned briefly at both of them. "When the clerk telephoned you were coming. Just said, 'Man and woman on the way up.'" Bill Weigand held the door open. "She's gone," he said.

Nan Schaeffer was not in it, but the suite of living room, bedroom and serving pantry was by no means empty. It was occupied by Mullins, by several other men in civilian clothes; by two uniformed patrolmen.

And all the rooms, the bedroom particularly, had evidently been searched. Drawers had been emptied, and clothing from them piled neatly on one of the two beds. Dresses had been removed from a closet and laid carefully on the other bed. In the living room, the contents of a desk had been treated with less consideration. Papers from it were strewn widely.

"Tell me about the call," Bill said. They told him.

"Like I said, Loot," Mullins said. "It's a snatch."

"Looks like it," Bill said. "It looks like she had come back and found somebody going through the place. And that whoever was doing it, decided to take her along when they left. That she got loose somewhere long enough to make a telephone call — you say she had called the police first?"

"Yes," Pam said. "She said something about not being able to make them understand."

Bill said, "Hm-mm," doubtfully, to that. But, if she was very excited, she might have failed to make herself clear. They would check. Then, she had called the Norths.

"Stein got me on the way home," Bill said. "He got onto Mullins, who's got everybody's address in his little book. And then onto the precinct, of course." What they had found was what the Norths saw.

Mrs. Schaeffer, according to the elevator man who had brought her up, had returned to the hotel a little after ten. She had gone up alone; whether, as far as the lobby, she had been with someone was unknown. No suspicious persons were remembered as having gone to the twelfth floor, but that meant nothing. The hotel was large; for a residential hotel busy. People briskly came and went, rode up and down.

"Door wasn't forced," Bill told them. "Somebody had a key that worked, apparently. That's not too hard to come by, if you're in the business."

"Burglars," Pam said. "But —"

Bill shook his head. He advised Pam to look around her. She did. She shook her head.

"Stuff from the drawers in the bedroom," Bill said. "Taken out, but stacked neatly. So things could be put back as they were. But, out here" — he indicated the living room, the rifled desk — "no effort to cover up. So?"

He waited.

"All right," Jerry said. "We're dumb, Bill."

147

"It looks," Bill said, "as if somebody had been searching for a specific thing. Had planned to leave things as they were found, so that nobody would know of the search. But, after Mrs. Schaeffer interrupted, there was no point in that, and reason for hurry. So — after the bedroom, they just dug in." He looked at them, seemed to study their faces. "A theory," he said. "So —"

The doorbell interrupted him. He crossed the room and opened the door and looked down at the woman who stood there — the small, trim woman with brown hair streaked dramatically with white. She looked at him.

"Why —" she said, and looked around the room, the rather crowded room. "What's happened?" she said. *"Something's happened to Nan."*

"Mrs. James," Pam said, from inside the room. "Something dreadful. Mrs. Schaeffer's —"

"Come in," Weigand said. "Mrs. James? Phoebe James?"

She came into the room. She wore a brown sealskin coat, held close around her; in the heat of the room she still did not release the clutched coat.

"I don't —" she said, and looked around again, and looked at Pam North. "I don't understand," she said. "Nan — what's happened to Nan?"

"Apparently," Bill Weigand told her, "Mrs. Schaeffer has been kidnapped. By someone she found ransacking her apartment. She telephoned Mrs. North and —"

"Telephoned you?" Phoebe James said, and looked at Pam. "But that isn't what I —" She stopped. She looked, Pam thought, taken aback; there was something almost of consternation in her expression.

"What you what, Mrs. James?" Weigand asked her. "What were you going to say?"

"Wait," Mrs. James said. "She telephoned you, Mrs. North, and — told you what was happening?"

Pam told her of the telephone call. When she had finished, Phoebe James said again that she did not understand it. She looked around the room. "This is so strange," she said. "So very strange."

"You expected to find her here?" Bill said. "Evidently you did. Had you arranged to see her? By telephone or some other way?"

"Arranged?" Phoebe James repeated. "They searched everywhere?"

"Yes," Bill said. He was patient. "Had you arranged to call on Mrs. Schaeffer tonight. At —" He looked at his watch. "At twenty minutes after twelve?"

"I hadn't arranged anything," Phoebe James said. "I — Forbes Ingraham was a very dear friend of mine." She seemed for the first time to see Bill Weigand. "You're a police officer?" she asked. Weigand identified himself.

"Of course," she said. "The officer Mr. and Mrs. North spoke about. Have so much confidence in. I was terribly upset, captain. I — I couldn't stand to be alone. I just came here on an impulse. To — to be with someone. You've felt that way?"

Bill nodded. He waited.

"That's all," she said. "Oh — to talk about what's happened, I suppose. To go over it and over it, and around and around in it. You think — 'perhaps there's something I forgot to ask. Perhaps there's something, some simple thing, we've missed.' Do you understand?"

Again Bill Weigand nodded.

"And now — this," Phoebe James said, and released her coat, moved her hands to indicate the room. "Nan — you really believe she's been kidnapped? Taken out of here forcibly? Or — or what?"

Everything looked, Bill told her, as if Mrs. Schaeffer had surprised intruders, been taken with them when they left.

"The men Forbes was — afraid of? Or wary of? The Norths have told you about that?"

"What she told them?" Bill said. "Yes. And — yes, that's a possibility. If they thought Mr. Ingraham had given her something. Something they might want. You think he would have done that?"

"I don't know," she said. "How could I know?"

"Or, that her husband had something they wanted. That she had brought it here when she moved after he died?"

Mrs. James merely shook her head. She shook it hopelessly. Then she asked if there was anything to indicate that Nan Schaeffer had been — she hesitated over the word — had been "hurt."

They had found nothing, Bill told her. He looked at her curiously. She did not seem to notice this. She shook her head again and as she looked around the room, her lower lip pressed between her teeth. Then she turned.

"There's nothing I can do, is there?" she said. "Nothing to help?"

"If you have any ideas?" Bill said.

"None," Phoebe James said. "I — it's the last thing I'd have expected to happen."

Then there was nothing she could do at the moment, Bill told her. It would be best for her to go home. Should he have someone go with her?

"Go with me?" she said. "Why? Oh — no,

I'm perfectly all right, captain. At least — I don't need anyone to take me home."

She held the coat around her. She looked at Pam North and seemed about to say something to her. But in the end she merely shook her head, and went to the door and out of it. Bill closed it behind her.

"Well," Pam North said, "I wonder what —"

The telephone rang. Weigand answered it, identified himself, listened. He said, "The hell it has," and listened again. He said, "Right, we'll be along," and replaced the telephone.

"The offices have been broken into," he said. "The law offices. Mullins!"

Mullins said, "O.K. Loot."

Weigand looked at the Norths.

"We," Jerry said, with firmness, "are going home. To sleep."

"Sleep?" Pam said. "With all this to worry about?"

152

VII

Wednesday, 8:20 A.M. to 11:45 A.M.

The cat was black, except for a white chest and one white forepaw. He sat tight against the front door, his tail wrapped close around him. It had snowed lightly during the night, and from his tracks in the snow it was evident the cat had been several times to the front door, and at least twice to the back door, and that once he had leaped to a window sill and, finding the window closed, leaped down again.

The cat shook his cold forepaws, first one and then the other. From time to time he cried out, in a voice which was plaintive, and angry, too.

It was Mrs. Isaacson who heard him most clearly. She lived next door, in a cottage very much like that which the cat sought to enter. Mrs. Isaacson was agreeably plump and rosy, and in her early thirties, and as she made the bed she sang contentedly to herself. She had been up before seven, and got her husband

153

up and off by seven-thirty. It is a long time from the center — the high center — of Staten Island to the tip of Manhattan. There is a walk to the bus, and a longish ride on the bus, and on the ferry one has enough time to read the New York *Times* from first to last, excepting the financial news. Larry Isaacson was due at the office at nine.

Mrs. Isaacson had washed the dishes and, since that was her day for it, cleaned the range. She had run the vacuum over the living room rug. Since these activities are not quiet ones, she had not heard the cat until she came to bed making. She did not, at first, pay much attention. But as the cat continued to cry, she began to notice the sound, and finally to wonder about it.

It was not like the cat to cry. She knew the cat well; frequently, in the summer, he dropped in for lunch. But he seldom had much to say, except what he said by purring. And now, quite suddenly, Mrs. Isaacson stopped, with a pillow tucked under her chin and the pillow slip dangling, and listened.

On a day like this — a cold, February day — it was strange for the cat to be out at all. In the winter, he was a dedicated house cat, and stayed where it was warm. Now and then he went out briefly in the morning, but by seven-thirty or thereabouts he was in again, and for the day. But now it was — it was eight-thirty.

Rose Isaacson put the pillow into the slip, and laid it on the bed. She went to the window, and looked across at the cottage next door. She saw the cat, flattened against the front door.

She raised the window slightly and spoke to the cat.

"What's the matter, Tommy?" she said. "You get locked out?"

The cat turned and looked at her. He spoke with increased vigor; he looked up at the door, then, and cried very loudly.

"She's not there, Tommy," Rose Isaacson said. "She must have gone —"

But then she stopped, and looked at the walk in front of the house and was puzzled, then concerned. There were the marks of the cat's feet in the snow — he had gone down the walk, apparently to look up and down the street, and come back again to the doorstep. But — there were no other marks in the snow. And the snow had been on the ground, in fact it had already stopped snowing, when Mrs. Isaacson had gone to the door with Larry, and his feet had left marks in the snow.

So her neighbor had not gone out, or had gone out before the snow fell or — had not come home? But during the evening, Rose thought, was almost certain, she had been conscious of a light going on there. Yes — it had shone in a window, interfering with television. She had pulled down the shade.

I do hope, Rose Isaacson thought, nothing's happened to the poor thing. It's not like her to leave the cat out. Particularly when the weather's so —

Rose put a sweater on. She went out her own front door and crossed to the house next door, her footmarks sharp in the light snow. The cat circled away from the door as she approached, and rubbed against her legs, and looked up at her, waiting. It had taken a long time for a person to see the obvious. The cat shook his paws, cold from the snow.

Rose Isaacson rang the bell and then, not sure she had heard it ringing, knocked.

"Mrs. Burton," she called. "Oh Mrs. Burton." When there was no answer, she called, "Are you all right?"

She tried the door, then, and it was locked. She tried to see into the house through the glass in the door, but white curtains cut off her view. She went to the side of the house, the cat following her, and found a window from which the curtains were drawn back. She could look into the living room, then.

She looked and the color faded from her rounded, pretty face, and horror sat in her dark eyes. She ran to her own house, and the cat ran after her, and into the house after her.

Rose Isaacson had forgotten the cat. She went to the telephone, and sat for a second, and took deep breaths to quiet her trembling. Then she picked up the telephone and dialed once.

"I want the police," she told the operator. "I want the police. The lady next door — I'm — I'm afraid something dreadful has happened —"

Captain William Weigand had got to bed at a little after four. He was at his desk at eight-thirty, feeling by no means as young as he once had felt. There was, he thought, hardly time left during which he could die young, as Dorian, his wife, had told him he was sure to do if he kept going the way he went. She had told him that in this morning's gloom, as she fed him breakfast. She had moved lithely in the room, and her eyes had been green (and indignant) and it had been difficult to think of murder.

Reports awaited on the desk. He was familiar with the contents of some, not surprised by the others.

The bullet taken from Forbes Ingraham's brain had so battered itself against his skull as to be useless for comparison, in case the opportunity for comparison arose. It had been fired from a thirty-two calibre revolver, from a distance of a few feet.

Forbes Ingraham had been a healthy man, until the bullet splayed against the frontal bone of his skull. There was no evidence of organic disease. "Well nourished, male; weight 160; height, five nine." There was no reason apparent why he should have sought medical treatment, which was confirmation, if needed, of his statement to Dr. Aaron Arn.

Fingerprints had been numerous in Nan Schaeffer's apartment. Hers predominated, as was to be expected. Almost as numerous were the prints of another woman, now identified as her personal maid. The fingerprints of the hotel maid were less widely distributed. There were prints, apparently less recent, left by Reginald Webb; he had left a clear set on the inside of a closet door, where his hand might have rested as he pulled the door open. In the laundry hamper was a shirt, also, from the laundry mark, left by Reginald Webb.

Matthew Halpern had not, so far as could be determined, left his hotel room during the night. This was to the best of knowledge and belief, both being supplied by two precinct men who knew their trade, and had during the night, followed it. If Halpern had been devious enough, he might have evaded observation. That went without saying, and was not said. It is seldom convenient for detectives to sleep in the same room with a man they follow.

A preliminary report from detectives of the Safe and Loft Squad was at hand, and for the most part it contained what Weigand already knew. The modus operandi was not distinctive, and Detective Rankin had reported as much a few hours before, as Weigand left the plundered offices of Schaeffer, Ingraham and Webb. "As a matter of fact," Rankin had said, "you could blow it open with a fire-cracker."

The safe had not been blown open. It had been opened by knocking off the combination. It had not been much of a safe; it was less of a safe now. It had yawned open when Weigand and Mullins first saw it; had seemed to leer at them, and at the others in the then brightly lighted, completely ransacked, offices. Files stood open; locked files had been jimmied open. Here there had not been, as apparently there had in Nan Schaeffer's bedroom, any attempt to hide the fact of search. It had been instantly apparent to the cleaning women who had got to the offices a little before midnight. They had notified the police; the offices had filled with the police.

Entrance had been made through the door leading to Samuel Schaeffer's former office.

The door had been forced. Judging by the thoroughness with which things had been pulled apart — individual deed boxes in the safe had been broken open, their contents scattered — the marauders had been around for some time.

The precinct men, and afterward the Safe and Loft men, had been unable to reach Reginald Webb. He was not in his apartment, or if there not in a mood to answer his telephone. Francis Cuyler had proved equally beyond immediate reach. "Keep late hours, these guys," Rankin told Weigand. Saul Karn had answered his telephone, but he had answered it in Mount Vernon. He was on his way in. It would take a while; it was snowing in Westchester and the roads were growing slippery.

The routine was almost finished when Webb answered his telephone and said, "Well, what is it?" to Sergeant Mullins. He sounded wide enough awake. Mullins told him what it was, and he swore and said, "Those damned thugs!" and hung up. He was at the offices in twenty minutes; had parked his car among the police cars in Forty-fourth Street, came to the door of the offices and looked in and swore again, at greater length. It was then two-thirty in the morning. He said, "I told Forbes to lay off that crowd," and then, to Weigand, "Well?"

"We've been trying to get hold of you for a couple of hours," Bill told him. "Wanted you here while we —" he looked over Ingraham's office, to which they had moved — "before we poked around."

He had been at his club, Webb said, and was abstracted as he began to pick up strewn papers, put them down again. "Old Mortimer's will," he said, and picked up a form from beside a broken deed box. "He'll have fits." He had played bridge at the club; when the game broke up, sometime around midnight, he had gone into the library and sat in a deep chair. "Tried to make some sense out of all this," he said. "You get hold of Karn?"

Bill told him about that.

"Somebody's had a busy night," Bill said then, and looked at the back of Reginald Webb, who was bent over a filing case, peering into it. "You've heard about Mrs. Schaeffer?"

It was as if Bill Weigand had hit Webb in the back, or had stabbed him in the back. The tall man straightened, turned, in a single violent movement.

"Nan?!" he said. *"What about Nan?"*

Before Weigand could speak, Webb took a long step toward him. "What's happened to Nan?" he said.

Bill told him. Webb's hands clenched as he listened; his eyes grew hot. "Good God," he said. "Oh, good God!" He raised clenched fists, lowered them again. "Nan," he said. "And I —"

Bill waited.

"This doesn't matter," Webb said, and his gesture included the office, its devastation. "What are you doing here? Why don't you look for her?"

She was being looked for, Bill told him. This was part of it — one thing would, almost certainly, lead to another.

"*You* —" Webb began, and Bill said, "Calm down, Mr. Webb. We'll find her."

"Alive?"

"I hope so," Bill said. "We're doing everything we can."

"I thought she'd be all right," Webb said. "I didn't see how she could be — how it could affect her. If I'd gone up with her — but she —"

"Gone up with her?" Bill said. "When, Mr. Webb. Tonight?"

"Sure," Webb said. "We had dinner and I took her to the hotel and told her to get some sleep and — *and went off and played bridge!*"

Bill told him he couldn't have known.

"Played bridge," Webb repeated. "Sat in

a deep chair and — pretended I was thinking things out. *Jesus!*"

He couldn't have known, Bill told him again.

But that was it, Webb said. He could have guessed. After the two men stopped him, threatened him. First that, then this — he indicated the offices — then, still looking for something, Nan Schaeffer's apartment. "But — why her?"

"They may have thought Ingraham confided in her," Bill told him. "Or that there was something in her husband's papers. What two men?"

"Didn't I —" Webb said and then, "of course not. I told Nan about it and was going to get hold of you, but —"

He told of the two men who had talked to him in the car. Said he could not identify either of the men. He could not give the car's license number. The men had guns, he hadn't felt encouraged to go behind the car and read the plate. He thought the car was a Chrysler — it was a sedan, dark in color — black, possibly dark blue.

"Listen," Webb said. "We're wasting time. Can't you see that? It's Nan who's important. I'm going —"

"There's nothing you can do," Bill told him. "Nothing we can't do better, aren't already doing. You can help here."

"While she's — you don't know what they'll do to her. You expect me —"

"Yes," Bill said. "What did they want here?"

"How can anybody tell? It'll take us —" he looked around — "hell, it'll take us weeks to find out where we are."

They had not, certainly, been after anything of cash value. There was no money there — possibly petty cash. Mary Burton would know about that. Otherwise, the cash register of the corner store would have paid them better. Here there were only papers. But there were hundreds of papers, thousands of papers. Those kept in the safe were, for one reason or another, of an especially confidential nature. "Were," Webb said, looking at strewn documents. Those in the locked filing cases were a little less restricted; the open cases held chiefly correspondence on current matters. "Jesus," Webb said. "I'm glad our clients can't see this."

Who would know most about what might have been searched for, might have been taken?

Mrs. Burton, in general. In matters particularly confidential, Saul Karn.

Karn had walked into the office at a little before three, precisely dressed and mannered, carrying a brief case, entirely wide awake. When he saw the office he removed his rimless glasses, shook them — rather as a physician shakes a clinical thermometer — and said, "My, my."

"Well," Webb said, "what do you think, Saul?"

"I imagine," Karn said, "that they were after this."

He opened the brief case. He removed from it a sheaf of legal sized yellow paper, folded twice. He handed the sheaf to Reginald Webb, who unfolded, and looked, and began to read the typescript. But after he had read half a page, he shook his head. He asked what it was all about.

Karn looked doubtful, looked at Bill Weigand, at Mullins.

"Mr. Ingraham considered it confidential," he said.

"Mr. Ingraham is dead," Bill told him.

"That is true. Nevertheless —" Karn looked at Webb. Webb hesitated. Then he told Karn to go ahead.

"Very well," Karn said. "It came to Mr. Ingraham's knowledge that certain conversations of interest — telephone conversations — might be made — available." He chose words with care. "A record was obtained."

Bill held out his hand. Webb gave him the typed sheets.

The conversations were dated, and timed; the first had been made on January sixteenth. The conversations appeared to be between one man, who in most cases seemed to have originated the calls, and several other men, identified by first names, by nicknames, in some cases not at all. Most of the conversations were cryptic —

"1-19; 3 P.M. — Nobby? Yeah, this is Joe. You see Mr. Painter? — Yeah. He's still squealing — So? — It breaks his heart, Joe. It sure breaks his heart. — That's too bad, Nobby. He came through? — What do you think? Sure he came through — That's nice, Nobby. That's real nice. — Ain't it. See you tonight, boss? — Sure thing."

"Joe," Weigand found, skimming from page to page, had talked with a good many men, with some of them often. "Nobby" was one of his more frequent interlocutors; he had conversed also with "Smiley," prosaically with "Jim" and "Tony," several times with someone named, improbably, "Horse." Most of the conversations dealt, directly or obliquely, with people, seldom clearly identified, who had "come through" or, in one or two cases, apparently had not. And once — on 2-1 — "Joe" had said, speaking to someone anonymous,

166

"Yeah, it's too bad about poor old Matt. Real tough."

"Right," Bill said, and folded the papers and put them in his pocket. "Who did the job, Mr. Karn?"

"The job?"

"Put the tap on."

"I understand," Saul Karn said, and spoke carefully, "that wire tapping is illegal, captain. I assume you mean wire tapping?"

"Yes," Bill said. "Who?"

"Of my personal knowledge," Karn said, "there was no wire tapping. No —"

"Please, Mr. Karn," Bill said. "Without prejudice, if you like."

"I don't know," Karn said. "Without prejudice, as you say — although the term is loosely used, captain — I would assume that someone was employed. If Mr. Ingraham knew, he did not confide in me."

"Ingraham hired someone?"

"I don't know."

"Or — was it Halpern? And turned the record over to Mr. Ingraham?"

"Again, I don't know."

"But you read this?"

"Yes. Yes, I read it, captain."

"What did you think it was?"

"It appeared to me that it might be a record of certain conversations between men engaged in a shake-down. That pay-offs were being made."

He did know the words, it appeared. He did not like them, but he knew them.

"You don't know who these men were?"

"No."

"But Mr. Ingraham did?"

"Presumably. And those who were employed to make the — recordings. And, I should suppose, Mr. Halpern. If he is the 'Matt' they mention, of course."

"You think whoever broke in was after this?"

That, Saul Karn said, would be his guess. The material had been in the safe.

"I took it out," Saul Karn said. "Took it home. To — lessen the risk, captain. Since the safe is by no means a new one and might easily be broken open." He looked at the safe. "I appear to have been right," he added.

"You know of nothing else they might have been after?"

"Oh, there may have been a dozen things. But — this seems the most probable. To me, that is. Perhaps Mr. Webb?"

Webb shook his head.

Bill Weigand had left the offices half an hour later, told Mullins to get himself some sleep, and gone home to get some sleep himself.

He had not got enough, he thought again,

and said, "Hello, Fred" to Sergeant Thackery of the Rackets Squad, who had come up from Headquarters on summons. "This is it," Bill said, and handed Thackery the results of illegal wire tapping. Thackery read. He said, "Well, well." He said, "Looks as if there might be something in Halpern's story after all." He read further. He nodded his head as he read.

"The 'Joe' would be Joe Smithson," he said. " 'Smiley's' a man named Bland — Smiley Bland. Not very appropriate names. 'Horse' I never heard of. Or 'Nobby'."

"But," Bill said. "You can find out?"

Thackery could. "This" — which was the conversation record — "would help." They could find out who had made the tap; with the guidance provided, they might find out a good deal.

"But —" Thackery said, "we haven't got anything they can't laugh off. You know that, captain. Nothing that'd be any good in court."

Bill nodded his head.

"So," Thackery said, "they go to the trouble of knocking off this lawyer? Searching the office — sure, maybe they didn't know what Halpern and his mouthpiece had and didn't want to take a chance. Maybe they got more. But — this mob's a little choosey about murder. Has been, anyway."

"Ingraham may have had more," Bill

169

agreed. "They may have got more — something Karn didn't know about, and so didn't take home. Ingraham apparently had something he was going to take to the D.A. His interest, and Halpern's, was the grand larceny rap, of course."

"Yeah," Thackery said, and stood up. "Well, we'll get on it, captain. See what the D.A. makes of this. Have a few little talks — with Joe and Smiley and this 'Horse' they talked to. See what we can stir up."

He might, Bill suggested, find out who Joe Smithson had been playing pinochle with the evening before. Thackery agreed that that figured, except that Smithson was more the poker type. "I'll get together with the Safe and Loft boys," he promised, and went to do it. Weigand returned to reports. The telephone rang. He said, "Homicide. Weigand." He listened, and his face set hard, but all he said was, "Right. We'll come over." He picked up Mullins in the squad room. Mullins saw his face, and saw trouble.

"Mary Burton," Bill told him. "Found shot in her house."

The body of Mary Burton lay on the rug of her living room, and lay in blood. But the blood had dried. The photographers had pictured the body, which would go into the records as "white, about sixty, well nourished." There was blood on the precisely curled white hair; Mary Burton's jaw had fallen as she died, and her face was longer than it had ever been. She had been shot, twice, once through the heart. She had worn a robe and a night-dress when she died. One in the morning was the assistant medical examiner's guess as to the time of death — his median guess. Between midnight and two a.m.

The homicide men of the Ninth Detective District had been working for a little under two hours. Acting Captain Flynn sketched for Weigand what they had, what it looked like.

The body found at about eight-thirty by Rose Isaacson, next door neighbor. Because of a cat. There had been snow on the ground, then. It had gone as the sun climbed. There had been no footprints in the snow, except those of the cat. Snow had fallen from three in the morning until about five, and not heavily. The murderer had come and gone, at the latest, some time before the snowfall stopped; probably, before it began.

The shots had not been heard by the Isaacsons, who lived closest, who lived very close. But this was possible, if the murder had taken place around midnight, the medical examiner's earliest allowable hour. It had been very windy then, and for about an hour before midnight and until just before the snow started.

"These places rattle and bang," Flynn said. "Live in pretty much the same sort of place. Rattle and bang. Wonder they don't blow down. A thirty-two doesn't make a lot of racket —"

"It was a thirty-two?"

"Yes. One slug went through her. Found it in her clothes. The lab boys have it."

"Usable?"

"Yes. Take a nice picture."

Also, the revolver could have been wrapped in something, which would diminish the sound of its discharge. Also, the Isaacsons slept soundly and with a window ventilator running. "So she says, anyway."

"She's a good witness?"

"Kind you dream about. Upset as hell, but mind keeps on working. Very nice little woman, Mrs. Isaacson. Says she was fond of the old girl, and acts like it. Says, 'It happened right next door and we didn't *do* anything.' I said I didn't know what she could have done."

"No," Bill said.

Mrs. Burton, who lived alone with her cat, apparently had got home about ten-fifteen, much later than usual. It was about then, at any rate, that she had turned on a light —

or someone had turned on a light — in her living room. The light had shone into the Isaacson living room until Mrs. Isaacson pulled down a forgotten shade. It had interfered with television reception, and television reception helped place the time. The light had come on, Mrs. Isaacson thought, in the middle of a show, and it was a ten to ten-thirty show.

"Yes," Bill said. "The cat?"

"Yelling to get in," Flynn said. "Spent the nights in. Altered cat. Didn't roam much. Probably went out when the murderer came in."

More probably, Bill Weigand thought, went out with the murderer. The cat would have been frightened, by then; would have hidden in a shadow against the strangeness in the night, would have fled from it as the door opened.

"Could be," Flynn agreed. "Don't know much about cats. Anyway, he got shut out. Snap lock on the door. Locked when the boys got here."

There was one other thing. A man of the neighborhood, coming home late from a lodge meeting, had seen a car starting up about a block away. He had seen, first, a man getting into the car; then it had started off. A sedan. He was not sure of the make, had no idea of the color, or of the license number.

173

"Didn't think anything about it," Flynn said. "Doesn't now. Much as he thought at all, he thought it was some guy who had been visiting his girl. Only — we haven't found anybody around there who had a visitor. Or, who went someplace that late in a car."

"Visiting a girl?" Bill said. "A young man, then?"

"That's what he thinks. He was about half a block away, and there wasn't much light. A thin man, he thinks — not very tall, either. Could have been some kid in his 'teens, this fella thinks. Fit anybody?"

It didn't.

"Could be," Flynn said, "that there's no tie-in."

"Trouble is," Sergeant Mullins said, with gloom, "trouble is nothin' ties in with nothin'. That's what makes it screwy. Like it always is."

Mullins did not specify the conditions under which it always was. He did not need to.

"Yes," Bill said. He spoke abstractedly, looking down at the cadaver which had been Mary Burton. He wondered what she had forgotten, or what she had remembered. Or, what she had had that was wanted, and wanted desperately.

There was too much in what Mullins said; events seemed, for the moment, as difficult

174

to relate one to another as the events of a dream. There were, also, too many events; it was as if a dozen maniacal children were playing, now here and now there, the grimmest of Hallow'een pranks, months out of season.

"Mrs. Isaacson's got the cat," Flynn says. "Says she's going to keep it, if nobody minds."

Bill Weigand looked at him.

"I don't suppose anybody'll mind," he said. "If it's all right with the cat."

Pamela North is an orderly person, among physical objects as well as among those of the mind. The latter characteristic has been brought in question, but not by Pam, who should know best nor, indeed, by her husband, who should know second best. The order of her mental processes is not, certainly, always of the simplest kind, but complexity is not, in itself, disorder. This day was to be devoted, at least in part, to the attainment of physical order, specifically of the things in her chest drawers, and to a final separation of Florida sheep from Northern goats.

She told Jerry this as he left for the office, with the urgent request that she not get involved in anything.

"I'm going to go through my drawers," Pam told him. "So of course I won't."

Jerry blinked slightly.

"Oh for heaven's sake," Pam said. "Chest drawers. Always the editor."

"Of course," Jerry North said, and kissed her, and said goodbye to each cat in turn, and left.

Pamela went at once to work, pausing only to skim the New York *Herald Tribune*, with special emphasis on Clementine Paddleford's food column, and to work the crossword in the New York *Times*. After a little thought, she decided to do her main closet as well, and first, so that Martha, when she came, could do a thorough dusting up. Pam opened the closet door wide, and began to carry garments from it. The dresses she stretched out, with care, on a bed, avoiding the creation of wrinkles. "I'd forgotten all about that one," she said to herself, and, of another, "I wonder what I was thinking of that day?" With the dresses ended, she shook her head dubiously, and thought that she didn't, really, have very many — not nearly enough. Not even with the things she had bought for the South, and which hadn't come yet.

There was almost a shelf of hats, and, of these, Pam tried several on. It always puzzled Pam to discover that she had so many hats, since she had, almost completely, given up the wearing of hats. She put the hats, one by one, with the dresses on the bed. She found numerous shoes, and sorted them into pairs — I really *am* orderly, Pam thought, in relation to the shoes, except that it doesn't always show — and pushed a fall coat and a spring coat and an evening wrap — I'll certainly never wear that again — to one end of the hanger rod. Now there was room for Martha to get in. After Martha had been in, the things which were going south could go here, and the things which were staying home could go there. I need a new wardrobe case, Pam thought; one that will really keep things nice. I knew I'd miss something. (This applied to a summer dress which she had planned to take south, but had forgotten to send to the cleaner, and for which it was now too late.)

With the closet completed, Pam turned to the chest drawers, and realized at once that it was some time since she had. Slips were folded, for example, but not really neatly folded, as one wishes such things to be. Pam was a little surprised at this, until she remembered that, several days before, she had needed a special slip — a blue one — and that it had been at the bottom of the pile and that, instead of lifting the whole pile up to the level of the blue slip, she had reached under it and —

Pam made a clucking sound with her tongue, and took all the slips out, and examined each — one for Martha to mend, when Martha had the time — and folded each and made a pile of them on the unoccupied bed. The blouses took longer and the stockings longer still, since stockings, once worn, often turn up unmated, on account of runs, and must be paired, which involves taking to windows for examination in natural light. But, in time, Pam had stockings sorted, and belts rolled, and bras and panties counted, and all things laid neatly on the bed. Pam sat down, lighted a cigarette and looked at them. All other things aside, including the need for at least two new dresses for the south, it did take a good deal to keep one woman covered. Spread out this way, with such careful neatness —

For an instant, then, Pam North experienced that disturbing feeling which all know — that this had happened before, precisely as now; that, indeed, it was, at one and the same time, happening before and happening now. One part of my mind isn't keeping up with the other part, Pam thought, and tried to hurry the laggard half. I hate this feeling, she thought, because when you don't know when you are, when are you? and —

But then, as instantly as it had come, the feeling of uncertainty in time took itself off. It isn't that at all, Pam thought. It's Mrs. Schaeffer's apartment at the hotel, and that's what's been worrying me, although until this minute I didn't know I'd been worried. That's what was wrong, out of drawing. It wasn't gangsters at all, Pam thought. *It was another woman!*

She put it in order in her mind, then, and as she did she nodded her head, with each movement impressing, as with a stamp, the validity of her thought.

If a man is looking for something, he rummages. He reaches under things and between things. His own shirts, for example, or all those things Jerry keeps in the top drawer of his own chest. (Pam had a mental picture of the top drawer, and shuddered, in an aside.) If a man — or men — had gone through Mrs. Schaeffer's garments, even if they wished to conceal the fact that they had gone through them, they would not have taken them out, and piled them neatly on beds. They would not have laid the dresses out carefully, extended, to avoid creasing, particularly since the plan had presumably been that they would all be hung up again. Men would have tossed the dresses on the bed if, indeed, they had not merely pushed them around on their hangers.

But a woman does not handle the fragility of clothing in this fashion — not even the fragility of another woman's clothing. Not, at any rate, a woman of — well, call it pride. Even a woman in the intermediate stage, as of the 'teens, handles party clothes with nice precision, whatever she may do about her dungarees. The most deft man — Pam thought with affection of Jerry — would lack some part of deftness. And gangsters were — of this Pam was certain — men with very heavy hands. (In motion pictures, they constantly knocked women around, to say nothing of their clothes.)

Then the person Nan Schaeffer had surprised in search had been of her own sex; had been, probably a woman who took pride in her own clothes, and her own grooming, and so would not wantonly mar another woman's. That she might, under the circumstances postulated, knock the other woman over the head with what came handy and then, in some manner not at the moment clear, make off with her, was entirely another matter. Faced with reality — clothes are, by intention, poetry — a woman does what she has to do, as a man does.

And, the disorder of the desk in the living room fitted too. Among such things, it is a woman's habit to rummage. Pam thought of her own desk and then, in further divergence, of the time she had left it open and one of the cats had got into it and, apparently, searched for a mouse. Pam had been upset, and almost angry; Jerry, viewing the scene, had remarked that the desk looked, to him, much as usual and, although this did not in any degree abate Pam's displeasure, she had been forced, in subsequent and calmer moments, to admit that Jerry had had something there.

It had been a woman, then, not the racketeers about whom Nan Schaeffer, from Ingraham, might have learned — and dangerously learned — more than she had said. Pam paused for an instant to consider, and reject, the theory that the racketeers might have used a woman. If it was as important as it would have had to be, the racketeers would have come themselves, at least two of them. They would have to erase the racketeers, and the realization that they would pleased Pam. She had never wanted it to be gangsters, whom she considered highly uninteresting. Presumably there were gangsters in it — she did not, except very briefly, toy with the idea that a woman had broken into the law offices — but they were not really of it. If they ran at all, they ran parallel, were only fortuitously involved. That had happened before; things are not all of a piece always, although it is convenient when they are.

Then something else, not evidence against union racketeers, had been sought. Then Nan Schaeffer knew — or had known — something else; something involving a woman. Presumably what she knew had had to do with Ingraham's murder. There could not be *too* many fortuitous circumstances. Then, a woman had killed Mr. Ingraham. Pam checked back to see that she had not made a demonstrable mistake. She discovered none. A woman had laid the clothing on the beds. The rest followed.

A name came up, as if in lights — Phoebe James. In love with Ingraham, and that love almost certainly her last. A love the dearer for its timing, the more jealously to be guarded. And — the less assuredly to be believed in. With Phoebe James, Pam thought, loves must have come and gone and so she must have realized that this would also go. A younger woman would appear, and for Phoebe James so many — so desperately many — women were younger. A time must come, Pam thought, when it is hard to let go, since you must fear you let go of all. And for a little snip of a thing, with blond hair —

I'd have hated Forbes Ingraham, Pam thought, and discovered that she was now actually hating him a little. To be loved by a woman like Phoebe James — and Pam now found herself acquiring a certain degree of devotion to Mrs. James — and leave her for a little snip of a thing, pretty certainly, but what else? Pam tried to check herself; admitted that she didn't know Phyllis Moore, and so had no real idea what else. She was unsuccessful; tolerance is all very well in its place. This was not its place.

Somehow, Nan Schaeffer had found something — a letter? or perhaps a gun? — which tied Phoebe to Ingraham's murder. Mrs. James had tried to get this thing, and Nan had surprised her and — *And afterward, Mrs. James had come back to go on with the search!*

I'll have to tell Bill, Pam thought, and reached for the telephone by the bed. But then she stopped. She tried to phrase the words of explanation, and her hand dropped from the telephone. Mrs. Phoebe James was proved a murderer because clothing had been piled neatly on two beds, not thrown helter-skelter, or merely rummaged through? Because, late at night, she had wanted to talk with a friend?

It was all right. It was perfectly all right. It was indestructibly logical. The only trouble was, it didn't sound so good. Even Jerry — well, even Jerry might think it didn't sound so good.

The thing to do was to get more before she said anything. And — to give Mrs. James a chance. Perhaps Mrs. James could explain or — or something.

VIII

Policemen walk a good deal. They walk from door to door, and ring doorbells and introduce themselves and ask questions. Patience is required, and comfortable shoes are desirable. It is frequently necessary to quieten those the sight of a policeman, even one not in uniform, excites, and time is so consumed. It takes half a dozen men, and the ringing of a great many doorbells, to establish with reasonable certainty that a young man walking to a car parked on a sidestreet in a Staten Island residential district and driving off in it, is not a resident going about the most lawful of activities — going home from having called on his girl; going off to start his night's work; driving down to St. George for medicine for a sick child.

Even after some hours have been spent, probabilities, rather than certainties, have been arrived at. There are always a few doorbells which go unanswered, even when rung

185

repeatedly; there is always a chance that somebody may, for reasons of tangential importance, be avoiding the truth. Perhaps some
young wife, her husband absent, has had a
visitor she would rather not explain. Perhaps
the parents of some girl have not been informed that their daughter is entertaining, in
their absence, a boy of whom they disapprove.
There are many possibilities to be considered.
Not all of them can be eliminated.

But by noon, it was the best opinion of the
detectives assigned that they could not identify
the young man who, in the middle of the night,
had got into a car a block from the home of
Mrs. Mary Burton and driven away, at no
great speed, being noticed in these activities
by Norman Slagel, insurance man, who was
then returning from a lodge meeting. (Insurance men keep up contacts. The work of an
insurance man is never done.)

Norman Slagel was a small, rather dark
man, and he occupied a small, rather dark,
office in St. George, Staten Island. Bill
Weigand talked to him there. Norman Slagel
said, "Gee, captain, I just happened to see this
guy. I didn't really look at him." It had been
some time since Bill had encountered a man
who said "Gee." One lived and learned.

But from Mr. Slagel, although he was very
willing to do what he could — after he had

pointed out, for the record, that he had already twice done his utmost — Bill did not learn too much.

"Nobody I ever saw before, far as I know," Slagel said, and was earnest. "And my memory's pretty good. Trained, you might say. In my business you got —"

"Right," Bill said. "A small man, you say."

"Not so small," Slagel said. "Not smaller than lots of people. My height, maybe. Maybe a few inches under. I wasn't paying much attention, because why should I? He came down the street —"

"Toward you? Facing you?"

"That's right."

"From the direction of Mrs. Burton's house, then?"

"Well, I didn't know the poor old girl. Know where she lived. But, from what these other cops — officers that is — tell me, I guess he was."

"The car was headed —?"

"Same way he was going. That is —"

"Right," Bill said. "Away from Mrs. Burton's house. Generally, toward St. George? Toward the ferry, I mean?"

Slagel agreed to that. Encouraged, he added details. The man had been slight as well as short — that was, if you called it short. Five feet three or four, Slagel would guess, estimating by his own five-six. The man had worn a snap brim hat; he had worn a loosely fitting coat, and it had swung a little as he walked. He had walked briskly. He had got in the car, and slammed the door, and the car lights had gone on. Slagel was within perhaps thirty feet of the car when it started, went past him, went on. The car had been a sedan. He thought a small Chrysler.

"Took it easy enough," Slagel said. "Not one of these jack-rabbit starters. Know what I mean?"

Bill Weigand did.

"Nothing to attract attention," Slagel said. "Just a young fellow getting in a car and driving off."

He was asked why he said "young" and puzzled over it, ended by saying he didn't know, that it was an impression.

"Sort of a bouncy walk," Slagel said. "Maybe that was it. Like he had a lot of energy. Fellow gets to be our ages, captain, he just sort of walks. Know what I mean? Young kid, he —"

"Right," Bill said, and was not happy. Well, it happened to everybody, of course. Particularly, Bill reassured himself, with inadequate sleep.

"You wouldn't recognize him if you saw him again?"

Slagel shook his head. He said, "Gee, I'm afraid not, captain." He paused. "Look, captain," he said. "I don't say I hadn't had a couple of drinks. You know how it is."

Slagel was thanked. Weigand and Mullins ate sandwiches at a counter; the launch took them back to Manhattan. A northeast wind was rising and the launch bucked it up the harbor, bounced into it. The sun which had melted the un-tracked snow in Mary Burton's front yard, on her front walk, was receding dimly into gathering clouds. Mullins, in comment, said, "Brrr." He asked Bill what he made of it, and Bill, absently, said, "Snow." Mullins looked at him, and realized he was not himself seen. The Loot was the way he got when he was, or thought he was, on to something.

"Bouncy," Bill said, after a long pause. "What do you think of, sergeant?"

Mullins said, "Huh?"

"Bouncy," Bill repeated. "A bouncy walk. What do you think of?"

"Somebody selling something," Mullins said. "Or — a guy with his hands on his hips." Still sitting, Mullins demonstrated the latter. He was not the man for it, but the demonstration sufficed. Bill grinned moderately in comment.

"The man's coat was swinging," Bill said,

after another pause. "A loose coat, swinging as he walked. A short man, not heavily built." He paused, and now looked at Mullins. "I wonder," Bill said, "what Slagel would have thought if he had seen this man walking away from him?"

For a moment, Mullins looked puzzled. Then he said he'd be damned.

"Not much light from the street lamps," Bill said. "Slagel wasn't very near. A snap brim hat, he said, which probably means it was snapped down — pulled down — over the forehead. Well?"

"Getting into the car," Mullins said. "You'd think that would tip him off. They're different."

The door was hinged on the forward edge. Hence it would open between Slagel and anyone getting into it. Slagel was still some feet from the car when it started up.

"O.K., Loot," Mullins said. "Could be."

"Right," Bill said. "And, it helps, doesn't it? Because none of the men — except Karn — is short. Or boyish, which Karn certainly isn't."

The launch circled in to the police dock. It tossed a line ashore and was made fast. Mullins and Weigand climbed from it, up a short ladder above tossing water, to the planking of the dock. Bill's Buick took them uptown, without benefit of siren. Bill parked it in a block on Forty-fourth Street, finding space between two other cars, in front of a sign which said "No Parking." The sign, a little plaintively, wore another: "No Parking Today."

"Well," Mullins said, "it doesn't say 'positively.'" They went up in the dignified elevator to the offices of Schaeffer, Ingraham and Webb. It was Phyllis Moore's pretty blond head, her pale and worried face, at the information window.

"Oh," she said. "Mr. Webb is just trying — Mrs. Burton hasn't come in and we can't get her on the telephone. Some man says she can't come to the telephone and —"

"No," Bill said. "I'm afraid she can't, Miss Moore." He looked at the pale, pretty face; saw strain in the wide blue eyes. "She's dead."

The girl put a hand up to her lips, and drew her breath in sharply, shudderingly. Dorothy Lynch appeared behind her. They were very much of a height, and both were slender — a little over five feet, each was, Bill thought.

"Dead?" Dorothy Lynch said. "You say Mary's dead?"

"She was shot," Bill said, and watched them. Mrs. Lynch was not as visibly affected as the younger woman had been. But her eyes widened.

191

"But — why?" Dorothy said. "Why?"

"I don't know, Mrs. Lynch," Bill said. He was patient. "I'm trying to find out."

Phyllis Moore said something Bill could not hear. "What?" he said.

"She must have seen him," Phyllis said, and now he could just make out the muffled, uncertain words. "When he —" But then she covered her face with both her hands, and backed away, shaking her head.

"Saw him?" Bill said. "Who do you mean?"

She did not answer, except again to shake her head. Her hands still shut out the world.

Bill looked at Dorothy Lynch.

"I don't know," Dorothy said. "She — she's afraid." She paused. "We all are," she said. "How can we help being?"

"I hope you needn't be," Bill said. "We'd like to see Mr. Webb, if we can."

They could; they did. He stood up behind his desk when they came in, and it was clear he sought calm. But his hands, resting on the desk, clenched nervously into fists. "I can't believe it," he said. "Now Mary!" and then he said, slowly, "Why?"

"She knew something," Bill told him. "Or saw something."

"Like — like Forbes? I mean, she was killed the way he was?"

Near enough, Bill told him. Shot as he had

192

been, with a thirty-two, as he had been. Bill waited; watched the tall man slowly shake his head.

"You can't guess," Weigand said, "what Mrs. Burton could have known? Or what she might have seen?"

"No," Webb said. "Unless — unless somebody going into Forbes's office. Someone she remembered afterward. That — well, that would have been like her. I told you that."

He had, Bill agreed.

"You haven't got anything? No clue?"

Bill hesitated, then. He let his hesitation be apparent. He appeared to make up his mind.

"A man was seen," he said. "A short man — thin. He was around — in the neighborhood, that is. He hasn't been explained. He had a car. But there may be no connection."

Webb shook his head, slowly. "Except Saul —" he said, and stopped.

"The man wore a loose coat that swung as he walked," Bill said. "A soft hat, canted down over his eyes."

"Oh," Webb said. "Not Saul, obviously."

"No," Bill said. "It doesn't sound like Mr. Karn. The man bounced a little as he walked, our informant says. Perhaps he might have picked a better word. But there was some movement he noticed. Made him think the man was very young." He paused. "Boyish," he said.

"Wait," Webb said. "What you're getting at —"

"Getting at?" Bill said. "That's the way he was described. As I said, we've no real evidence he —"

He stopped. Webb was not looking at him. Webb was looking over him, through him; looking as if at some distant, frightening thing. His eyes were blank, for the moment. His hands unclenched and clenched again. It was brief, and Webb started, as if wakening.

"What about Nan?" he demanded, then. "What are you doing about Nan Schaeffer?"

"What we can," Bill told him. "We have been all night. Are now. Things take time."

"Time enough for her to be killed," Webb said. "Like Forbes. Now like Mary. Why? For God's sake — *why?*"

He was told they didn't have the answers yet. All the answers.

"Any of them," Reginald Webb said, and leaned forward across the desk and his voice went up. "You don't have *any* of them. Some kid goes home from seeing his girl and you — *my God!*"

"Take it easy, Mr. Webb," Mullins said. "Take it easy."

"Take it easy till you find Nan's body,"

194

Webb said. "Find hers like the others. Then you've got another answer." His tone was violent. "You don't know where you are. What you're doing."

"It's been twenty-four hours," Bill said, and his voice was very quiet. "Thereabouts. We're doing all we know to do. If somebody wants Mrs. Schaeffer dead — well, yes. She's dead by now. But, if they wanted her dead, why not kill her when she walked into her apartment? Ingraham wasn't given any chance. Mrs. Burton wasn't." He paused. "Mrs. Schaeffer means a lot to you, doesn't she?"

"She's an old friend. She —" Webb stopped. "All right," he said. "She means a lot to me."

"Since her husband died, I take it?"

"Yes. But take it any way you like. What are you working on? Helping Dr. Kinsey?"

"Take it easy," Mullins said. "Just take it easy."

"Right," Bill Weigand said. "As the sergeant says, Mr. Webb. We're wasting time. You're wasting ours. We want to find out where people were last night. You've told us where you were. The others haven't. At the time Mrs. Burton was killed."

Webb said he couldn't stop them. He sounded as if he would like to. They saw Dorothy Lynch, first. She had been at home, been in bed. "With a husband in the next bed,"

195

she said. She was a little shaken, but under control. Mary Burton had said nothing the day before, when they left the evening before, which, looked back on, helped. "She was terribly broken up, poor thing. She kept crying and shaking her head. As if she weren't thinking clearly."

"And Miss Moore?"

"Like the rest of us. Upset. We had enough, didn't we?"

"Yes," Bill said. "Did Mrs. Burton say anything to her, do you know?"

Mrs. Lynch did not think so.

"You have no idea — no idea at all — what Mrs. Burton could have known about Mr. Ingraham's death?"

How could she? Dorothy Lynch asked, and Weigand could not tell her. They let her go, and waited for Phyllis Moore; waited in Saul Karn's office, and Karn, evicted to the library, placed marking slips neatly in legal volumes. Phyllis Moore came in and was very pale; her lipstick had a kind of violence on her curving lips, which now trembled just a little.

She had gone home the evening before, when they had let her go. Home was in White Plains, in a two-room apartment. She did not share it with anyone. She had stopped, late, at a little restaurant she knew — a restaurant called Le Pingouin Gai, where the food was admirable and not expensive. She had driven there from the station, from there driven home.

She had a car? She appeared momentarily puzzled by the question. Of course she had a car; if you lived outside the city, commuted, you needed a car. Buses took forever. The kind of a car? A small sedan. A Chevrolet.

"Why all this?" she asked, not with antagonism evident, but seemingly in perplexity.

They had to ask many things, most of them not relevant. Mary Burton had said nothing to her — nothing that, seen now in perspective, might help? She had not.

"No one else? You went straight from the office to the train?"

She hesitated, then, and the hesitation was evident. They waited.

"Mr. Cuyler," she said. "He — he asked me to have a drink. Said —" She hesitated again. She's making it up, Bill thought. "Said he thought I needed one," she finished, and then looked quickly, too revealingly, at Weigand, then at Mullins. Do you believe me? her eyes said, her waiting expression said.

They did not.

"You had a drink with Mr. Cuyler," Bill said. "Caught your train? Had dinner at this restaurant? It must have been a late dinner."

"About nine," she said. "A little after. It's

only half an hour by express."

"Yes," Bill said. "And got home — around ten, say?"

"I think so."

She had gone to bed about eleven; had got up at seven-thirty, come to New York and the office. When Mary Burton had not come by ten, she and Dorothy Lynch had not been greatly worried. "Everything has been — not the way it usually is." But when she still had not come an hour later, or called in — then they had told Mr. Webb, and, at his instruction, called Mrs. Burton's home. And — and heard she could not come to the telephone.

"Right," Bill said. "To go back, Miss Moore. Yesterday, from the office, Mr. Ingraham made a telephone call to the district attorney's office. You have no idea about what?"

"How could I?"

"You weren't on the switchboard."

"No — Mary — do you think I'd have listened?"

"Mrs. Burton was on the switchboard?"

"Yes. But he just asked for an outside line. She spoke about it afterward because — I suppose she felt he didn't — well, trust her. But she wouldn't have listened. None of us would."

She was steadier, now; better controlled.

"You and Mr. Cuyler had a drink together," Bill said, and his voice was sudden. "Was that unusual?"

"Why," she said. "I don't —" Her eyes widened; she looked quickly at Bill Weigand, and more quickly away. "Why shouldn't —?"

"You're hiding something, Miss Moore," Bill said. "Not very well, either. What was special about your having a drink with Mr. Cuyler?"

"He — nothing. Nothing at all. He thought I needed one."

She looked again from one to the other.

"There wasn't anything else," she said. "Really there —"

"You must have talked about Mr. Ingraham's death."

"We — I suppose so. I don't remember what we talked about."

"Speculated about who had killed him. Whether whoever it was went in from the main office, or through the back door. Wondered — wondered *why*, Miss Moore. You must have talked about that."

"I — I don't remember."

"Why don't you? It was only last night. A man you'd known for several years, worked for, is murdered. In an office just across a corridor." Bill watched her. "A man you liked, Miss Moore. You did like him? Older, of course — but he had a good face; people seem to have liked him. He had a soft, friendly voice, people say and —"

She had been sitting near the desk. She leaned toward it now, put her arms on it, dropped her head on her arms. She moved her head from side to side, as if she sought, so, to escape from something which hemmed her.

"Don't," she said, "please don't. Please. Please." Her voice was muffled. "I can't —"

"Or wasn't he that kind of man? Were people wrong about him? Maybe that soft voice of his wasn't real. Under that gentleness — did you hate him, Miss Moore?" She did not seem to hear. "Did you hate him?"

That brought the blond head up, the blue eyes wide. Then color came suddenly into her pale face.

"Why do you say that?" she said. "He — he wasn't like any other man who ever lived. I'd have done anything — anything in the world — to keep him from being hurt. And because I felt that way — because of me — of *me* — this awful thing — this awful thing —"

She stopped.

"You were in love with him?"

"Francis says it wasn't — yes, I was in love with him. And he wasn't in love with me.

Not the least bit. I was just — just a pretty enough girl who was a pretty good stenographer. He was kind and — oh, he tried to make it all right. Fixed it so I worked mostly for Mr. Cuyler — or Mr. Karn — so — so I'd get over it. And —"

But again she stopped speaking, and then there was a kind of blankness in her eyes.

"You said because of you. What did you mean, Miss Moore?"

She shook her head, then. She shook it slowly, each movement seeming calculated, seeming final.

"Is Francis Cuyler —"

It was as if he had been waiting for this moment behind the closed door to the office, listening behind it.

"Is Cuyler what?" Cuyler said, at the opened door. The girl did not turn. "So," he said, "you got around to it, Phyl. I didn't need to be afraid you'd go to the police, did I? That's what you said. Remember? Because — how could you? Well — you found out how, apparently."

The girl did not turn. She spoke flatly.

"No," she said. "I didn't find out how. I —"

"Well, Mr. Cuyler?" Bill Weigand said. "What did Miss Moore get around to?"

Cuyler stood very tall just inside the office

201

door. He pushed his black hair back from a broad, white forehead. The gesture was dramatic; seemed a prelude to dramatic speech, possibly in blank verse.

"Come off it," Cuyler said. " 'What did she get around to.' What are you trying to give me?"

"Miss Moore has told us you and she had a drink together last night, after you left the office. Because, she says, you thought she could do with one."

Cuyler pushed again at his hair, although now there was no need. He stared at the back of Phyllis Moore's head, at its shining blond cap. She did not turn. "That's all?" Cuyler said, finally, and the question seemed to be to the girl.

"All that had to do with you, Mr. Cuyler," Bill Weigand said, when the girl said nothing. "But now —"

"Now I've walked into it?"

"Right," Bill said. "I think you have, Mr. Cuyler."

Francis Cuyler shook his head, seeming to chide himself.

"All right," he said. "I thought you were bullying the girl."

"Did you?" Bill said. "Well?"

"All right," Cuyler said again. "She thinks I killed Ingraham. Said so last night. When

I made her. She's nuts — nice, but nuts. Not a very bright girl. I told you that last night, didn't I, Phyllis. Nice and pretty and not very bright. She said she wasn't going to say anything — just keep it our little secret. I thought she'd changed her mind."

"No," Bill said. "She hadn't. That's why you bought her a drink?"

"Why?" Cuyler said. "Oh — in a way. To get her to come out with it. She'd gone around all afternoon looking as if she were penned up with Dracula or somebody. For a dumb girl she's got quite an imagination. For —"

"Don't keep on saying that," Phyllis Moore said, without turning. "Just don't keep on saying that."

"Well," Cuyler said. "She can talk. Think of that."

The girl turned, then. She looked at Cuyler fully, slowly. Her face was puzzled again. She seemed surprised, and to be waiting in surprise.

"I told you I didn't," Cuyler said. "You didn't listen, but I told you. Also, you didn't drink your drink."

She merely shook her head to that, and the gesture might have meant anything.

"You just confuse people," Cuyler said. "You —"

"Wait," Bill said. "You accused Mr. Cuyler

of killing Mr. Ingraham. Is that right, Miss Moore?"

She did not take her eyes from Cuyler's face. She nodded her head.

"On what grounds?" Bill asked her. "Something you saw?"

She still did not speak, and after a moment Cuyler laughed briefly.

"Good as your word, aren't you?" he said. "No, she didn't think she saw anything, captain. Or — didn't say that, anyway. It was something else, wasn't it Phyllis?"

She still said nothing, still waited.

"Thought I was jealous," Cuyler said. "Because of her. Because of the play Ingraham was making for her — pretending not to; teasing her along, just the same. Being fatherly and —"

"No," Phyllis said. "It wasn't like that. It wasn't that way at all." She turned, then, to Bill Weigand. "I told you how it was," she said. She turned to Cuyler. "I did tell them that," she said. "Nothing about you."

"However it was," Bill said. "Were you jealous, Mr. Cuyler? I take it you deny killing Ingraham."

"You can," Cuyler said. "About the other —" He again ran a long hand through black hair. "I'm a damn fool," he said. "But — all right. Ingraham got in my hair. I as good as

204

told him that day before yesterday. Told him I was quitting, that I was going to try to take Phyllis along."

"Take her along?"

"As a secretary. She's all right at that. Never think she's dumb about — other things."

"Ingraham took it all right?"

"*He* took it all right. Or pretended he did. This little — this pretty Phyllis, she wasn't having any. Sure, I could go. I gathered that would be fine — But she was going to stay as long as Ingraham wanted her to and — oh, the hell with it. She made me mad." He looked at her. "Real mad," he said. He shook his head. "All the time," he said, "I know one girl's like another, or near enough. What's so damn special about you?"

"Nothing," she said. "Nothing's special."

"Not a damn thing," he said. But his face did not repeat his words, and his black eyes did not. He seemed, for that second, to have forgotten Weigand, forgotten Mullins. Except for the girl, the room was empty. This did not last; he seemed to break from it. He turned to Weigand.

"All right," he said. "You've got your answer. I didn't kill Ingraham. I don't much mind his being dead. So?"

He was not particularly antagonistic. He waited.

205

"Where were you last night?" Bill asked him, and then Cuyler seemed surprised. He had had dinner, alone; he had gone, still alone, to the residential hotel in which he lived. He had read awhile and gone to bed, probably about midnight. He seemed puzzled.

"Mary's dead," Phyllis Moore said. "She was killed last night. The way Forbes was."

Francis Cuyler swore then, not loudly. He shook his head. "Who the hell," he said, "would want to hurt the poor old thing?"

They couldn't tell him that, Bill Weigand said. A general guess was easy — she had known something. A more specific guess — Bill shrugged.

"You've got nothing?"

They had some things. Bill told him of the discovery of Mrs. Burton's body, of the wound which had killed her, of the bullet found.

"The same gun?" Cuyler asked, and then Bill temporized, said they did not yet know, that tests were being made. That tests were not being made, since they would be useless, was something for the police to know. Bill hesitated, then, as if debating with himself whether to tell more. Finally, he told of the young man — the slim young man with a bouncy walk, a top coat which swung with his movements, who had been seen in the vicinity; seen driving from it. He did not question the sex of the person who, if "bouncy," might have taken short steps, moved hips in a certain fashion.

The question apparently did not, for Cuyler, arise. He listened, in the end shook his head, the gesture signifying that it was all too deep for him, too obscure for him. And with that, it seemed that he dismissed the matter, perhaps as outside his province. His eyes went back to the girl, who now sat facing him; who now was not so without color in her face, who was looking at the tall, black-haired man as if he wore some disguise she must penetrate.

"The description doesn't suggest anyone?" Bill asked, after the pause had lengthened.

"What?" Cuyler said, and seemed to return from a distance. "Oh, that — no. I can't say it does. Nobody I know."

They had got no further when, a few minutes later, they left the office. Bill was not sure that either of the two was fully aware that the police did leave it, although Cuyler made a gesture, said something about being around if wanted. He and Mullins had not, Bill thought, really held their audience, toward the end.

"She's about the right size, all the same," Mullins said, in the library, outside the door of Saul Karn's small office. "And he's got it bad. About her."

"Right," Bill said, and watched Saul Karn enter the library from the corridor. Karn was also the right size; he was not, however, to be described as bouncy. He walked precisely toward them, and removed his rimless glasses and waggled them, also precisely. He said that this was a dreadful thing about poor Mary, and was agreed with. "It appears she must have known something," he said, and was told it did. He presumed they had questions as to his whereabouts at the crucial time and, for the record, they had. He had been at home, in Mount Vernon, with his wife. He had been asleep when summoned to the office to survey its devastation. They were surprised only that he had a wife, and this surprise they concealed.

"I have something here you might want to see," Karn said then. "A letter. I came across it this morning while going through the documents. We felt — Mr. Webb and I — that you should see it."

He held out, then, a single sheet of paper, folded, and from the look some time folded. It was a letter, written in long hand, addressed to Forbes Ingraham, care American Express, Paris, signed in hieroglyphics. "Mr. Schaeffer's signature," Karn told them, and gestured at the letter, now in Bill Weigand's hand.

"Dear Forbes," Weigand read. "Glad to hear you're getting a few days to amuse yourself. About our position on the Commonwealth rights, I agree completely. Our friend Fergus is an impatient little man, but he always is. I've put him on the back of the stove, pending your return. It'll do him no harm to simmer.

"Poor Mary got me a connection in Portland Oregon yesterday when I wanted one in Portland Maine. Situation normal, as the boys say. Mine is also, but I'm taking it a little easier than usual, on suggestion. Not running for subway trains, and that sort of thing. Of course, I haven't run for a subway train for years, but I do as I'm told. You begin to, at my age.

"We'll expect you on the eighteenth."

The signature, Samuel Schaeffer's if Karn said it was, followed. Bill Weigand shook his head.

"You think it means something?" he asked. "What, Mr. Karn? Mrs. Burton's mistake? But — didn't she make a good many? Or is there something significant in Commonwealth rights, or this —" he refreshed his memory — "the impatient Mr. Fergus?"

Karn shook his head. The Commonwealth rights had to do with clearance on a motion picture, based on a client's book, being made in England. Mr. Fergus was another client. Karn's glasses brushed him aside, or chopped him down.

"The contents of the letter," Karn said, "are entirely trivial. They appear to be entirely irrelevant. And that is rather the point, isn't it? Since Mr. Ingraham had locked it up in the safe, instead of filing it. Or, for that matter, throwing it away after he received it."

"In the safe?" Bill repeated.

"Precisely," Karn said. "Among the things disturbed last night. Which is an unexplained circumstance, I felt — and Mr. Webb agreed when I raised the point. A letter of no importance, brought back from France by Mr. Ingraham, carefully locked up, as if it were of considerable importance."

Weigand looked at it again. It was dated early in December; if the eighteenth mentioned was of that month, the letter had, presumably, been sent air mail.

"Unless, of course," Karn said, "a matter of sentiment was involved. Presumably, Mr. Ingraham received the letter about the time, or perhaps after, we were forced to cable him of Mr. Schaeffer's death. But, that does not seem to me an entirely adequate explanation." He looked up at the ceiling. "No," he said, "not really adequate." He looked again at Bill Weigand. "None of us here," he said, "was aware that Mr. Schaeffer's health was in any way impaired."

The small, precise man seemed to feel a

point was made. The point escaped Acting Captain William Weigand.

"Mr. Schaeffer died in an accident," Bill said. "So I gathered, at any rate."

"Quite," Karn said. "Precisely, captain. Mr. Schaeffer fell downstairs."

Once more, Bill Weigand read the letter from Samuel Schaeffer to his partner — his last letter to his partner.

"You and Mr. Webb discussed this?" he said.

"Mr. Webb," Karn said, "agreed with my suggestion that, because of the circumstances, it had better be shown to you."

Bill nodded slowly.

"Asked me to give it to you," Karn said, "since he was leaving for the day."

Bill looked at him.

"Why yes," Karn said, "Mr. Webb left about twenty minutes ago. I presume he had an engagement."

IX

Things had not, for Pamela North, worked out as anticipated. To began with, it had at first proved impossible to get Phoebe James on the telephone. Pamela had tried at noon; the hotel switchboard, after a brief pause, had regretted that Mrs. James did not answer. After a further pause, it had discovered that Mrs. James had gone out, was expected to return at one.

There are few things more aggravating than to prepare oneself for the pounce, only to discover that the quarry is beyond reach. Any cat will agree to this; Martini, consulted after Pam had replaced the telephone, appeared to. She would, Pam told Martini, merely have to wait. But, prepared for movement, she had found inaction trying, and waited only some ten minutes. She had thought then that one might get some shopping done in an hour or so, and taxied uptown to try it. There had been only time for two pairs of resort shoes

212

and a new bathing suit; no time at all to try on the summer print so enticing on the mannequin. Pam had made a mental note of the print and, at one-fifteen, again telephoned Mrs. James's hotel. She got a maid, this time; then Phoebe James.

"I wondered —" Pam began and Phoebe James said, "I hoped you'd call. Can you come and have lunch with me? I've been frantic about Nan."

Pam could; Pam did. Mrs. James herself opened the door, and did not lack poise, although there was worry on her handsome, intelligent face. They had sherry, very dry and very pale, before a low fire, and lunch afterward, and nothing was as Pam had envisioned it. From the beginning, Pam felt herself off balance, having found no opportunity for the pounce. The tension for which she had prepared herself was not much in evidence. "Frantic" had, apparently been only a manner of speaking. Mrs. James, although they talked of kidnapping, and of murder, remained poised — too poised to be pounced upon.

"It's really frightening," Mrs. James said, but she spoke slowly, her voice low, controlled. "First Forbes. Now Nan. I can hardly believe it about Nan."

"I know," Pam said. "To walk in like that and —" She waited.

But then Mrs. James diverged. She said she lived two lives and that now, with this outer life so difficult — "so tragic" — she felt that she lived neither.

"All morning," she said, "my people were strangers. The people I know best. Do you understand what I mean?"

Pam shook her head.

"Your husband would," Mrs. James told her. "The people in the book I'm writing. All morning the people outside — Nan and these racketeers — kept jostling in." She sipped from her glass, refilled it, and refilled Pamela's. "You'll think I'm unreal," she said. "I get you here to talk about Nan — about all this dreadful thing, and I talk about myself. The man I loved is dead and one of my best friends disappears, and I spend the morning worrying about what a woman named Daphne — I don't know why I named her that, either — would say to a child whose father had left them both — not what she would say, but the words she would use." She shook her beautifully shaped head, with its dramatic streak of white. "Tomorrow morning, I'll tear it all up," she said. "It's wrong."

"You were here?" Pam said. "All morning? Because I telephoned earlier and they said —" (But I'm off the track, Pam thought.)

"Oh," Phoebe said. "I was here. But that's

a rule — until one, I'm never here. I should have given you the other number."

Pam waited, and she explained. The mornings were for work, and the hotel switchboard had instructions. There was, however, another phone line, which did not go through the switchboard. The number was known to few: to a literary agent, to a publisher and two magazine editors; to a few friends. "Write it down," Phoebe insisted, and Pamela — after a somewhat prolonged search through her bag, found a stub of pencil (somewhat chewed, since Pam had taken up cross-word puzzles) and the back of an envelope with space left for a telephone number — wrote it down.

"About Mrs. Schaeffer," Pam said, putting her hands firmly, as she hoped, on the steering wheel. "You came there last night to —"

"Talk," Phoebe said. "Reginald called me. He's telephoned everybody — everybody who knows her. He's — I suppose you could say he's beside himself. Whatever that means. Do words worry you, Mrs. North?"

"Well," Pam said, "not particularly."

"Clichés," Phoebe said. "They're so elusive, often. 'Beside himself.' I mean he's disturbed. Anxious. Why didn't I say that?"

"I don't know," Pam said. "Why is he?" (Again, she's put me off the track, Pam thought.)

The question seemed, momentarily, to surprise Phoebe James.

"Didn't you —" she began, and then said, "But why should you have known?"

"Oh," Pam said, in a certain fashion.

"Yes," Phoebe James said. "That's the way it is. Has been for — oh, a year and a half. Two years. But, the strange thing is — not lovers. At least, while Sam was alive. Nan says that and — I believe her. That's odd, isn't it? If it's true, it's odd. That I should believe it, odder still. Because, nobody believes in innocence. There's no benefit of any doubt any more, is there?"

"Well," Pam said.

"So Reg Webb's world is upside down. And mine is — both mine are. A woman named Daphne — I'll change that name — is stricken dumb. And — I'm not." She shook her head. "I'm certainly not," she said.

They had been finishing lunch, by then. The maid removed dishes, brought coffee and small, colored pastries. Pam succumbed to their bright temptation; Mrs. James did not.

"I'm not always this way," Phoebe said, after the maid had gone. "I'm — well, I'm flying apart. You know those sparklers — Fourth of July sparklers — how the sparks shook every way? I feel like that. Not so

216

bright, not so gay. But like that. Or — like crying."

She did not seem near tears; her voice remained quiet, under control. It occurred, momentarily, to Pam, that Phoebe James was talking of another Phoebe James, and that both — the observer and the observed — were beyond access.

"I don't always talk so much," Phoebe said, now. "What were they looking for at Nan's? What do the police think?"

Pam did not know. She thought the police did not. Presumably, something which bore on Forbes Ingraham's murder. Presumably, then, something Ingraham had given her — or was thought to have given her — at his office, the day before he was killed. Presumably, then, something concerned with, and revealing of, Halpern and the union, and the racketeers. Perhaps the same thing the (presumably) same people had sought in the law offices. Did Mrs. James know about that? She did. Reg had told her. She shook her head, hopelessly.

"At Mrs. Schaeffer's," Pam said, "things were taken out of drawers. In the bedroom. Piled up neatly. You weren't in the bedroom?"

"No. You know that."

Pam described the bedroom; described it

slowly, carefully; watched Phoebe James as she talked.

Mrs. James listened. She seemed to listen carefully. But if she was enlightened by what she heard, or surprised by it, or frightened by it, none of these responses was revealed in her expression. When Pam finished, Phoebe James said only that they must have been looking for something small, and this was not at all the right answer. Pam had expected a guilty start, at the very least. (She has always wanted to observe one.)

"You don't see anything strange about it?" Pam asked, after a pause had lengthened.

This did elicit what appeared to be surprise.

"Strange?" Mrs. James repeated. "Strange, my dear? Isn't it all — strange? If you want to use such an inadequate word."

"Everything in neat piles," Pam said. "The dresses carefully spread out. Why neat piles?"

Phoebe James shook her head, and seemed perplexed.

"Neat men?" she suggested, as one responds in a guessing game.

"That's it precisely," Pam said. "Don't you see? Not men at all. Men would have burrowed." She paused, again waited response. "Like woodchucks," she said, helpfully.

Mrs. James did not appear to be helped. She looked at Pam North, her eyes widened.

218

"Women," Pam said. "Don't you see? A woman, anyway. Piling things up neatly so they wouldn't be mussed. A woman who — who just couldn't help doing that. Probably hardly realized she was doing it. A woman who couldn't — just *couldn't* — paw things around."

The eyes which had opened widely at Pam North's previous remark, now narrowed slightly. After a moment, Phoebe James nodded her head, slowly. She said, slowly, not with certainty, that she did, now, see what Pam meant.

"It's a small thing," she said. "Not conclusive, but — have you talked it over with anyone? Mr. North? Your policeman friend?"

"No," Pam said. "I — I just thought of it."

"And," Mrs. James said, "telephoned me. Why, Mrs. North?"

"Oh," Pam said. "Why — because I wanted to see what another woman thought of it. And — and because you asked Jerry and me to help. And —"

"And," Phoebe James said, "because I'm perhaps the kind of woman who doesn't, as you say, 'paw' things? Or, you assume I am? And — wait — you think I came back, not to talk, but — *to finish up?*"

"Well," Pam North said.

"You're impetuous," Mrs. James said. "Very impetuous, aren't you? Does it ever get you into difficulties, Mrs. North?"

"Difficulties?" Pam said. "What kind of difficulties?"

Mrs. James shook her head at that. She said that Pamela North was not stupid, and said it so that the words had the quality of an accusation.

"You get a notion in your head," she told Pam. "That a woman was involved in kidnapping Nan. You think — 'could it be Mrs. James? Who admits she was in love with Forbes Ingraham. Knows that a younger and prettier woman was' — how would you phrase it, Mrs. North? — 'making passes? Making passes at Forbes Ingraham. Says she knows the passes got nowhere, but that's only what she says.' Isn't that what you thought? That I might have killed Forbes. Then, because she knew something, Nan Schaeffer. But tried to make it appear that these gangsters had kidnapped her. And so — you come here to find out. Come alone. Or — did you tell somebody you were coming?"

"Why," Pam said. "Of course I — of course I did."

"No," Mrs. James said. "I asked that, remember? If you'd talked it over with your husband. Or the police. You said you hadn't.

220

And — you drank sherry I offered you. And food I served."

"We both —" Pam began, and stopped. She remembered a pastry. It had been a very pretty green pastry. Pistachio, it had been. Surely it was pistachio? Not —

"So nice not to have to watch your figure," Phoebe James said, with serenity. "To be able to eat pastries. I haven't been able to for years. But, of course, I've lived much longer than you have, haven't I?"

Why does she phrase it that way? Pam thought. What — what an *unpleasant* way to phrase it. As if — Pam did not believe any of this. She assured herself she believed none of it. It was much cooler than it had been in front of the low fire. It was almost chilly.

"You see where impetuosity might lead, don't you?" Mrs. James asked her, in a very pleasant tone.

Pam leaned forward a little in her chair. She looked, intently, into the other woman's face.

"You're — what do they say? Getting your own back," Pam said. "Aren't you?"

"If you want to think so."

"Because it's all so very — so very made up," Pam said. "So full of holes. The maid. The man at the desk downstairs. I wasn't sure of your room number, and I asked. The el-

221

evator man. He said it looked like more snow. The —"

"There might be ways of filling the holes."

But then Phoebe James smiled slightly, as if at a joke of her own. Pam was not certain that she knew she had smiled so.

"Mrs. James," Pam said. "Were you here last night? At" — she paused, remembered — "at eleven-fifteen?"

"When Nan was kidnapped," Phoebe James said. "You're persistent, aren't you?"

"No," Pam said. "When she telephoned me. Because — she'd telephone you, wouldn't she? An old friend. Probably she knew the number of your private telephone. But — she had to look my number up, didn't she? Why didn't she call you?"

"Perhaps she did," Phoebe James said, slowly. "Perhaps — will you believe me if I say I was here? Until — oh, about midnight? When I went to her place — found the police there?"

"Why didn't she call you?"

"As I say, perhaps she did. But — I'd taken the receiver off. Told them downstairs not to put any calls through on the line from the switchboard. I had to try to think. But — things got worse and worse. Then I went to Nan's."

She spoke flatly. She looked intently at Pam North.

Then the telephone rang. It was very loud, it sounded violent, as if there were suddenly a great hurry about something.

Phoebe James had to walk the length of the long room to the telephone. She walked quickly, and with grace. She picked up the telephone and said, "Yes?" and then, "Wait! I can't — Nan?"

There was a brief pause.

"Nan!" Phoebe James said again. "I can't — where are you, Nan?"

Again she was silent, her face intent.

"Listen," Phoebe said. "*Listen, Nan!* We'll come. You call the police. We'll come." She hung up. She almost ran back up the room.

"Come on," she said. "*Nan!* We've got to go to her. She says — she says they're coming back!"

Pam hesitated. Phoebe James was at a closet by the door; she jerked a coat from a hanger and a handbag from a shelf; she was at the door.

There seemed no time to think. Pam went after Phoebe James.

Dr. Arn was at the hospital. At the hospital, he was in surgery, not available. He would be told, when possible, that Captain Weigand had called. Bill Weigand drummed with his fingers on his desk top; he looked out through a small window, which could have done with washing, and discovered that it was now snowing heavily in West Twentieth Street. The telephone rang, and he answered it; he said, "Go ahead, Thackery."

Detective Thackery of Rackets went ahead; he was succinct. They had been too late in seeking the man named "Smiley" Bland; "Horse" — "man named Horsman it turns out to be" — had galloped. "Anyway," Thackery said, "they're not where we looked, and we looked in the right places." They looked still; Bland and Horsman would be found, eventually. That went without saying; Thackery did not bother to say it. For the moment —

Joe Smithson had taken a morning plane to Miami.

"Guess he don't like cold weather," Thackery said. "He took a woman with him. Have we got enough to have them picked up when they land?"

"No," Bill said. "I haven't, anyway. You identify the woman?"

They had not. It was not Smithson's wife. "Or his regular girl." Both remained in New York; Mrs. Smithson ostensibly indifferent; the "regular girl" expressing eager desire to get her hands on that two-timing so-and-so. "Looks like something's sort of messed up his love life," Thackery said, in a tone of no regret.

All they knew about the woman was that she was wearing a mink coat which looked like money. (Told of that, the "regular girl" had amplified her description of Smithson, filling in a number of gaps she had left in her first impromptu remarks.)

"Little under medium height," Thackery said. "Nice figure. That's all we've got so far."

"Nothing to indicate she wasn't going willingly?"

"To Miami?" Thackery said. "This time of year? Why — oh. You're thinking of the Schaeffer dame? The one who was snatched?"

The Schaeffer dame had, Bill admitted, crossed his mind.

"The woman with Smithson wasn't kicking and screaming," Thackery said. "Not 'sfar as we know."

"Right," Bill said, and thanked Detective Thackery of Rackets and suggested they hold Horse and Smiley, on whatever charges came to mind, when Horse and Smiley came to hand, that they send him photographs of all three. But that had already been done, Thackery told him. Bill hung up, drummed on his desk top again, told Mullins, at another desk, that Records was taking its own sweet time, as usual, and called the Fourteenth Precinct.

He learned that Matthew Halpern had left his room at seven-thirty, crossed the street for breakfast at a diner, walked to his office; that he was still in his office. Nobody had bothered him; he had not, so far as they knew, bothered anyone. Eyes were nevertheless being kept on him.

Weigand drummed again on the desk top. A messenger brought an envelope containing photographs and Bill looked at them. The telephone rang. It was Staten Island, this time, reporting nothing in particular to report. The bouncy youth was still unlocated. They had tried the ferry and got, "Listen, I don't have to *look* at them" from the man who, from midnight on, had collected from ferrying motorists. Widened enquiries in the neighborhood in which Mary Burton had lived and died had added nothing to what they knew.

"How's the cat?" Bill asked, and got a surprised "Huh?"

"The cat who found the body," Bill said. "Or, helped find it."

"Oh, that one. Last we saw, it was sitting on the doorstep. Making a good deal of noise."

"Yes," Bill said. "Right. Thanks."

He waited again, his fingers drummed again. He looked out through the small window at the snow.

(The Loot's jumpy, Mullins thought. Looks like we're getting places.)

The telephone rang again. This time it was Records. Bill listened; he made notes. It took some little time. Bill said, "Yes," three times and "Right," once. He said, finally, "The company paid? No squawk?" and when he was answered, said, "Hm-m-m." He said "Thanks" and replaced the receiver. Mullins waited.

"Accidental death," Bill said. "Fell downstairs, as Mr. Karn said. At his apartment. Little before midnight, December fourteenth. Duplex apartment. Got up to go downstairs for something and stumbled."

Schaeffer had died of a broken neck. There had been no injuries not explained by the fall. He had been sixty-five years old. He had been five feet eight; weighed over two hundred pounds. The precinct detectives had no hesitancy in noting "Accidental Death" on the record. There had been no autopsy.

"Let's go, sergeant," Bill said. Mullins said, "O.K. Loot," but he looked puzzled.

"To the scene of the crime," Bill told him.

Not until she reached the street was Pam North really convinced that she was making a mistake — possibly the mistake of her lifetime. Leaving Phoebe James's apartment, in

Phoebe James's wake, caught up in Phoebe James's urgency, Pam had had no time to think. Nor was there, then, anything to arouse alarm, and there was much to quieten it. In the carpeted corridor, softly bright, assurance that all was well, since all was comfortable, was almost automatic. In the elevator, more brightly warm, faintly fragrant with the mingled perfumes of well provided women who rode snugly up and down, there was nothing alien. But on the sidewalk, under the canopy, doubts rapidly arose.

It was snowing and snow in the city of New York impels almost anyone to look on the dark side of things. It had been about to snow when Pam went into the hotel, but about to snow is another matter; there is always a chance that it will not. It was snowing heavily, now, and the snow blew under the canopy with savage intent. It was after four, and dark — glumly dark, grayly dark. The doorman, who had been sheltering himself in the doorway, went out with his head shaking in doubt, and with his ears covered with small slip-covers, and whistled into the gloom. He'll never get one, Pam thought, and was thankful. But he got one almost at once.

"Wait," Pam said, as Phoebe James urged her into the cab. "Oughtn't we — the police —"

"Come on," Phoebe James said, and it occurred to Pam that she was being pushed. But then Mrs. James was beside her and the door was closed on them, and Mrs. James gave a number in the far east Sixties to the cab driver. They were, Pam realized, going almost to the river.

"She'll call the police," Phoebe James said. "Only — there isn't enough time. It might take them hours."

"Minutes at most," Pam said. "Surely you know —"

"Then they'll get there first," Phoebe said. "That'll be fine. Driver, can't you go faster?"

"In this, lady?" the driver said, and stopped, skidding a little, in a line of stopped cars. "Sit back and take it easy, lady."

But Phoebe James sat on the edge of the seat.

"You haven't told me anything," Pam said. "What did she say? What happened? Listen — I don't even know where she is."

"Where she used to live," Phoebe James said. "They took her there. I don't know why. She wasn't coherent. Kept saying they were coming back. You didn't hear her?"

"No," Pam said. "No, I didn't."

"She'll tell us," Phoebe said. "If we're in time."

The cab started up again. Mrs. James sat forward on the seat, as if by leaning forward she could force the cab to greater speed. She seemed to strain forward.

She changes so fast, Pam thought. In the apartment she was quiet, controlled. Now — I wouldn't think any other woman would be so important to her, Pam thought. Not any *woman*. I don't know anything about her. If Jerry was killed, Pam thought, would I be as she is — like — like a clock running fast and slow, with hands now whirling, now almost stopped? As if whatever governs a clock's speed were broken?

She looked at the intent face beside her, seeing it in profile. It was a strong face. Was there a sort of ruthlessness in it? Pam shivered. Unconsciously, she edged a little away from the other woman. The cab stopped again. I could reach out and open the door and get out of here, Pam thought. But she could not do that; not until she knew. Nan Schaeffer needed help. I wish I had never got myself into this, Pam North thought, and then thought, what have I got myself into, really?

She tried to sort it out. Nan Schaeffer had telephoned, from the apartment in which she had lived before her husband died. The men she had surprised in her hotel suite the night before had forced her to leave with them, and had taken her to her former apartment and — and left her there, with time to telephone?

After they had told her they were coming back?

"Why did they leave her?" Pam asked Phoebe James, and Phoebe, without turning, said, "What? I don't know. I told you I didn't know."

But then, as if unconsciously, she put a hand out and gripped Pam North's wrist. The pressure of the hand was unexpectedly strong. Pam moved, and the grip seemed to tighten.

How do I know it was really Nan Schaeffer? Pam North thought. If she'd been speaking loudly — hysterically — wouldn't I have heard the voice, if not the words? Even from the other end of the room. Was it someone else? Did she arrange, after she knew I was coming, for someone else to call at a certain time, so that she could pretend it was Nan Schaeffer and get me — here with her? Going to — to this place which must be almost *in* the East River?

The cab had crossed Second Avenue. It was moving more rapidly, now, through streets less crowded.

She knew I suspected her, Pam thought. I told her I did, or as good as told her. And — *she warned me.* Said I was impetuous. Perhaps she thinks I know more than I do — because I don't — I didn't, anyway — do anything but guess. Perhaps Nan Schaeffer knew more, as I thought, and — and isn't waiting for us, somewhere, but is — *dead somewhere!*

She moved. The grip on her wrist did not change. "We're almost there," Phoebe James said.

"You're hurting my wrist," Pam said.

Mrs. James turned and looked at her, and said, "What? I —" But she looked down, then, at her own hand, gripping a slender wrist. "Why," she said, "I didn't — how awful of me. What a strange thing for me to do."

She released Pam's wrist. She smiled at Pam, faintly, as if in apology.

"I must," Phoebe James said, "just have wanted to make sure — make very sure — that I wasn't alone. Because — I'm not brave. Not really. Not brave at all. If you hadn't happened to be there — when Nan telephoned — I don't know what I'd have done." She shook her head, and looked at Pam, intently.

"I've never done things like this," she said. "Never in my life. Just written about them."

She wrote historical novels, Pam remembered. Pam did not often read historical novels, but it occurred to her that there is a good deal of violence in most of them — a good deal of violent death.

X

Wednesday, 4:25 P.M. to 5:20 P.M.

The house was on a corner; it was on the last
possible corner. The cross street dead-ended
beyond the house; a reflecting sign gave final
warning, an iron railing blocked the unobser-
vant from a plunge to the busy drive below,
or to the East River. Now, there were fewer
cars on the drive than usual; lights of tugs
in the river were hazy through the snow, and
the water-craft hooted sadly at one another.
The northwest wind had full sweep here, and
made the most of it. The driven snow was
not soft here; here it seemed half sleet.

The house was dark. "This what you want,
lady?" the cab driver said, as if doubting it.
"It's what you said."

"Yes," Phoebe James said. "Oh yes," and
had the door open, had a bill out of her purse.
The driver, paid, said "Thanks, lady," and
almost before Pam and Phoebe James were
out of the cab, swung it in a u-turn and went
away — went back toward light and the fa-

miliarity of crowded streets. Pam shivered, and followed Mrs. James, who was across the sidewalk, at a door in the center of the house. There was another door, to the right as one faced the house, almost at the corner of the house. There were tall windows on either side of the center door, and they were dark.

There was a little light from a street lamp on the corner. Toward it, Phoebe James held her opened purse, searching it; toward the light, after a moment, she held a key case, keys dangling. She seemed uncertain for a moment, as if choice were difficult. But then she said, "This is it," and held one key alone and turned to the door. She turned the key in the lock and then, as the door opened inward, reached out for Pam's arm. They went through the door almost together, and Pam had only time to think of holding back before it was too late to hold back.

It was warm inside — warm and dark, and Phoebe James said, loudly, "Nan? Where are you, Nan?" Her voice had a hollow sound in what was, evidently, a large room — her voice seemed to echo from emptiness. "Here somewhere," Phoebe said, in a lower voice — but not low enough, Pam thought; not nearly low enough; it was a time to whisper. Phoebe was groping along a wall; there was a click and light went on — light high above them in a two-story room, an enormous room.

"Nan!" Phoebe James called again, and again she was unanswered. She found another light switch, and lamps went on, and now the room was merely a large room, comfortably furnished, with tall windows on their left — the river side of the house, Pam realized, without thinking — with curtains which hung straight from distant ceiling to floor.

"But she's not —" Phoebe James began, and turned toward Pam, and her eyes were wide. Then they heard a faint sound; a voice which seemed to come from a distance, to be muffled by distance, and by walls and closed doors. "The library," Phoebe James said, and went across the big room. Pam went after her.

A steep staircase of ornamental iron angled upward across the wall they faced, projected out from the wall, with only a single iron column supporting it at its highest point. It led to a balcony, from which two doors opened. But Phoebe James did not lead them to the stairway, but under it to a door, off center, near the bottom of the steep iron stairs. The door opened toward them; opened into a corridor, with doors on either side. Light showed under the nearest door on the left and when, once more, Phoebe called Nan Schaeffer's name she was answered, faintly, from behind

235

the door. "Here," the voice said. "I'm here — in here."

The room was not large, but it was large enough for a desk, and an easy chair, and a heavy sofa. It was by the sofa, on the floor, that Nan Schaeffer lay, a telephone — the receiver out of its cradle — beside her. "Oh," Phoebe said, and was across the room, on her knees beside the slight, bound woman.

There was nothing of Nan Schaeffer's immaculate grooming left, now. Her dark gray suit was crumpled, her short hair in disorder. On her right temple there was the discoloration of an ugly bruise, and in the center of the bruise there was dried blood. And her ankles were tied together with heavy cord, and more cord wound about her body, pinioning her arms. She drew her breath in and out quickly, convulsively, as Phoebe, kneeling beside her, kneeling between her and Pam, tore at the knots.

"Get a knife," Phoebe said, over her shoulder. "In the kitchen. Across the hall."

Pam went. The first door opened on a closet, empty except for two coats on hangers, and Pam slammed it shut. The second opened into the kitchen; the light switch was near the door jamb; knives were in the second drawer Pam opened. She ran back across the hall, holding a paring knife.

But it was evident that Phoebe James had worked efficiently without a knife. Nan Schaeffer was sitting up, the upper part of her body free. She held herself upright with her arms extended behind her and seemed dazed. She watched Phoebe working on the knot which held her ankles bound. The knife aided, there.

They helped her to the sofa. They got her water, first; then, from a cabinet under the steep iron staircase, brandy. She kept saying, "I thought nobody would come. I thought nobody would come."

"Wait," Pam said, as Phoebe said, "You need coffee. I'll make some coffee," and started toward the door. "Wait," Pam said. "The men who did this. Didn't you say they were coming back? Hadn't we —"

But Nan was shaking her head. She seemed, now, to be emerging rapidly from the shock which had been, minutes before, so evident.

"The lights," she said. "You turned the lights on. They'll know somebody's here. It'll be all right, now."

"And," Phoebe said, "the police will be here. You called them, didn't you, Nan?"

"The police?" Nan Schaeffer said. "Oh — yes. I called the police. My head hurts. They hit so hard. Did I tell you?"

She seemed, again, uncertain. She swayed

a little, on the sofa where she sat, and Pam sat beside her, and told her that everything was all right, now, and agreed that there would be time for coffee — and listened for the sound of police sirens, which at any moment must scream in the blustery night, scream through the heavy walls of the house. It was a little puzzling, Pam thought, that the police had not got there first. The police were quick.

"This will work wonders," Phoebe James promised, when she brought the coffee. It was a homely phrase, and a hopeful assertion. But it did seem to work wonders. After she had drunk a cup, accepted another, Nan Schaeffer seemed much clearer in her mind. She touched her bruised temple gently, and said "Ouch," and managed to smile. "I'm much better, now," she said. She looked from one to the other of her rescuers. Doubtfully, she stretched arms and legs. She said, "I wondered if I'd ever be able to move them again. They tied the cord so tight." Phoebe looked at her. "You saw," Nan Schaeffer said, and Phoebe nodded slowly, then said, "Yes."

"What did they want?" Pam asked, then. "Or — probably you'd better wait."

Nan shook her head, at that. She said, "I don't know what they wanted. I still don't know," and then, "They talked about a list. They went through Sam's desk —" she indicated the desk — "and started to pull out the books. I wasn't tied up then. That was later."

"It would be clearer," Pam said, "if you started at the beginning. Started with last night."

"Of course," Nan said. She seemed anxious to make it clear. "I'd been to dinner with Reg and he took me back to the hotel and I went up, and —"

She had opened the door, and found the living room dark. She had stepped inside, and reached to the side for the light switch, and then the lights went on before she touched it, and the door closed behind her. They had, she supposed, heard her key in the lock, and been waiting just inside the door.

One of the men had a gun, she told them — a small gun, she thought a revolver. He had said, "Take it easy, sister," and had pointed the gun at her. The other man had done most of the talking, although not much talking was done.

They had not struck her then. That came later. Nan Schaeffer told her story slowly, looking, as she spoke, now at Pam North, now at Phoebe James.

She had not gone out of the living room of the suite. She had been ordered to sit down, and had sat down on a sofa. The man with the gun stood in front of her, with the gun ready. He had been a man of medium height, dark, with a small tight mouth. The other man, who was somewhat taller, had gone into the bedroom and been there about five minutes and come out. He had shaken his head.

"All right, lady, where is it?" he asked, Nan told them. She seemed very much herself, now; her voice was steady; she chose her words.

"I said I didn't know," she told Pam and Phoebe James. "I said I didn't know what he meant. He said, 'The list, lady. Where's the list?' I still didn't know what he meant, and told him I didn't. He said, to the other man, something like, 'She don't know much, does she?' and the other man — the man with the small mouth — said, 'Maybe we could help her.' It was —"

She stopped, as if she had remembered something then, as she spoke.

"A small mouth," she repeated. "One of the men who — who threatened Reg — had a small mouth. Reg said so; he said it was the only thing he could use in describing them. These must have been the same men. But — why?"

She seemed to seek an answer in their faces. She did not find it.

It was strange the police didn't come, Pam

240

North thought. They always came so quickly.

The taller of the two men had shaken his head, Nan told them, to the suggestion — the threatening suggestion — of the man with the small, tight mouth. The taller man, who seemed to be the one who made decisions, turned and started to go through the desk. It had been, until then, apparently untouched.

"What he wanted must have been something written down — really a list of some sort," Nan said. "He went through everything. He worked very fast, but he looked at everything."

"Wait," Pam said. "Wasn't there a woman with them?"

Surprise was evident in Nan Schaeffer's face. "A woman?" she repeated. "What makes you ask that? There wasn't any woman."

"Not in the bedroom?" Pam said. "She couldn't have been in there? Where you wouldn't see her?"

"There wasn't any woman. The door was open. I could see into the other room. Why do you ask about a woman?"

"I thought —" Pam said. "I made a mistake, apparently. Go on, Mrs. Schaeffer. What happened then?"

(But, as Nan, after shaking her head, as if puzzled, went on, Pam looked not only at her, but at Phoebe James, also. Mrs. James was watching her friend intently and now and then, just perceptibly, she nodded her head at something Nan Schaeffer said. It could be — of course it *was!* — the movement so many people make as they listen to show that they do listen. It could not be — of course it could not be! — a gesture of approval, a way of saying, "You're doing fine. You're getting it all right." As — as a teacher might nod, finding a pupil letter perfect. . . . Why *don't* the police come? Pam North thought.)

The list had not been in the desk. "How could it have been? I don't know what list they were talking about." The taller man had given up, in the end. He had stood beside the man with the gun and looked at her. He had said, "All right, lady. Where'd you put it?"

She had denied, again, knowing what he was talking about. The man with the small, tight mouth had shaken the gun in his hand, shaken it in warning, turned to the other man and said, "Well, what d'you say? Help her remember things?" But the taller man had, again, shaken his head.

"Where'd you go this afternoon, lady?" he had asked. "Maybe you can remember that."

She had.

"I told him I'd been at your apartment," she said, to Phoebe James. "With Mr. and

Mrs. North. Before that, here. I've still got some things here," she told Pam. "Things I forgot, or didn't think I'd want. I told him I'd had dinner with Reg, and where. The taller man said — I remember now, I didn't pay much attention then — he said, 'So you were the date, huh?' I should have realized then he was one of the men who talked to Reg — made him get in the car."

"They brought you here," Phoebe James said. It was not a question. (But why should it be? Pam thought. Of course they did. She *is* here.)

They had made her walk between them, Nan Schaeffer said. The man with the gun kept it pressed against her. They had taken her, not to one of the passenger elevators, but to a service elevator at the end of the corridor. "I never knew where it was," she said. "Even that there was one. But they did." The elevator was automatic. They took her down in it, to a floor below the lobby floor — a place of harsh concrete, without comfort. They had taken her through a door and along a corridor, and through other doors. They had met a few people — waiters, she thought; hotel maids. But nobody seemed to pay any attention to them. "They all seemed so hurried." They had taken her out, finally, into the street, through what appeared to be a service door.

A car had been waiting; they had put her into it, and sat one on each side of her, and a man who had been waiting in the car, behind the wheel, had been told where to drive.

"What time was this?" Phoebe asked her. "Do you know?"

It had been, she thought, about eleven o'clock when they reached the street. She was guessing; she thought it had been a little after ten, certainly not later than ten-thirty, when she had entered the apartment and found the men there. She did not think it was more than half an hour, perhaps less, when they took her out. It had taken not more than five minutes to reach the building — the two-apartment building — in which she had lived with Sam Schaeffer, in which now she told her story.

Nudged by the gun, she had found the key to the apartment and opened the door and —

"Wait," Nan said, interrupting herself. "They sent the other man — the driver — some place first."

After they had got out of the car, she said, she and the man with the gun had moved toward the street door of the apartment; the other man had leaned in the front window of the car and talked, briefly, to the man there. She had not heard what he said, but thought the driver had been given instructions. Then —

But again she said, to herself, "Wait — I remember something else. Just a couple of words — something the taller man said to the driver. He must have raised his voice. It was something about a ferry. If he wanted to make the ferry, or he had better make the ferry — I don't know."

"This driver," Pam said. "Could the driver have been a woman?"

"A woman?" Nan Schaeffer repeated, and the surprise in her voice was this time very evident. "Why do you keep — no, of course not. A man was driving — hardly more than a boy, really. He had that thin back of the neck boys have, and narrow shoulders. I didn't see his face. But of course it was a man. Or a boy. Why do you keep asking about a woman?"

"She thought," Phoebe James began, but Pam said, "It doesn't matter. I had a — it doesn't matter. They took you inside? The man with the small mouth. The other man. Surely you can describe the other man?"

"I don't know," Nan said. "I'm — I'm afraid I'm no good at that sort of thing. A good many people aren't. He had — a hard face. His eyes — I think they were brown. There wasn't anything to remember — like the other man's mouth, small and tight."

"You'd know him if you saw him again?" Pam asked her.

"Oh — if I saw him. Probably I would."

(I sound, Pam thought, like a detective — like a policeman. And — where were the police? A long time ago they should have —)

"Mrs. Schaeffer," Pam said. "You *did* call the police?"

"The police?" Nan Schaeffer repeated. "I told you — I tried to get them and — it was all confused — and then I tried Phoebe and —"

"Not then," Pam said. "Now. Or, just before now. Before we got here."

"Of course," Nan Schaeffer said. "I — of course I did. Phoebe, and then the police. They said they'd — they'd send someone."

"They haven't," Pam pointed out.

"You think they're so quick," Phoebe James said. "They're not — you see now they're not. I told you that."

"But —" Pam said, and then, "All right." Probably it was all right. Anyway, the men hadn't come back. With lights in the house, they wouldn't come back. Nan Schaeffer was right about that. "How did you get a chance to telephone?" Pam asked. "Not this afternoon, although — anyway, I mean last night. When you called me? Jerry and me?"

She had, Nan told them, been taken into the living room and told to sit down, the small-mouthed man pointing out a chair with his revolver. The men had locked the street door and begun to search the big room. They had started with her desk — "it's over in a corner; it's more a table than a desk, really — a table with drawers." Finding nothing there, they had begun to search the cupboards.

Pam repeated the word.

"Two of the walls are panelled," Nan said. "Didn't you notice? Behind the panels are shelves to store things — cupboards. You tap the walls in certain places, and the panels open. We —" She broke off; momentarily her face worked. "Sam and I used to keep all sorts of things in them," she said. "Books and papers, and one section was for liquor and —"

The men had become engrossed in their search. Nan Schaeffer, after twenty minutes or so, had thought she saw a chance. She had stood up and, when they did not stop her, had moved toward the rear of the room, and the door under the staircase. She had stood there for a moment and then, still thinking herself unnoticed, had gone through it.

"I think now," she said, "they let me go thinking I would lead them to whatever they were looking for. Or, perhaps they really didn't notice."

247

In any event, she said, she had managed to get to the library. "This room." She had got to the telephone, and tried first to get the police. She had got somebody and been unable to make him understand. Probably, she said, she hadn't been very coherent — the man had kept saying, "Wait just a moment. You're talking too fast." But she had not, she decided, time to wait. She had hung up, and then dialed Phoebe James's private number. She had not turned on the light, knowing the number, being able to see the dial in the faint light which came in the big window. And Phoebe had not answered.

"I — I was desperate," Nan Schaeffer said, and now she leaned forward, and her manner seemed to reflect the desperation of the night before. "I tried to think of somebody who would be home — I didn't think Reg would have gone straight home — I thought of you, Mrs. North — you and your husband. I had to turn a light on to find the number, but I put the lamp on the floor and —"

She recreated the scene, as much by her manner, her quick gestures, as by her words. Pam could see her, crouched on the floor, shielding the light as much as possible, turning frantically through the flimsy pages of the telephone directory, finding the number she sought, listening to the sound of ringing —

and at the same time for a sound behind her.

"When you answered — your husband did," Nan said, "I — I couldn't keep my voice down. You know what I said — probably you remember better than I do. Because — almost at once one of them came in. I tried to talk fast, to tell you where I was and — I didn't get it out, did I? Of course I didn't."

"No," Pam said.

"He hit me," Nan said. "With the gun, I think. It was as if something exploded in my head and then — then I don't remember. I was knocked out, of course." She touched, very gently, the bruise on her temple. She said she supposed she was lucky to be alive.

When she was conscious again, it was dark in the room — "this room, they left me here." She could hear them moving in the room outside and after some time they came into the library. They drew curtains and turned on a light, and came over and looked at her. She had opened her eyes; she closed them. But she had not, apparently, been quick enough. "She's coming out of it," the smaller man said. "Want I should —?"

Nan had, she said, opened her eyes at that, and the man had raised the revolver, to use it as a club. But the other man said, "Hold it. Maybe we can do better," and had gone out of the room. He had returned in a few minutes with a glass of water, and a bottle of sleeping pills. "My own," she said. "I — I couldn't sleep after Sam — but when I moved, I left them here." They had made her take two capsules. Almost at once — "I suppose I was still groggy" — things had begun to seem unreal, and she could not be sure what was happening.

But during that growing vagueness, before she again lost consciousness, she thought one of the men had used the telephone. She did not know which man. "They were both — shadows." One "shadow" had used the telephone; had dialed a number, when answered had said, "Well?" She thought he had said nothing more, then, but had listened. After some time, during which all, for Nan Schaeffer, grew more vague, the man had said, something else, and again she thought she had caught the word "ferry."

"But I can't be sure," she said. "Not of anything then."

It had been daylight when she awoke, to find herself lying on the sofa. At first, she had thought the reason she could not move was that she had lain too long, in a position too cramped. But then she realized she was bound. And she could hear sounds from the living room, and realized the men still were there. After a few minutes — she thought it was a few minutes — the men had come into the room and, once more, stood and looked down at her. She had not, she said, pretended to be asleep.

"She'll do," the taller man had said, after looking at her carefully.

"And then he said, 'Just take it easy, lady. We'll be back.' Then they both went out and — I guess — left. Oh yes — they got the keys out of my purse. It was on the floor."

She still, she said, had no idea what time it was, but finally she had twisted herself around so that she could see an electric clock on the desk. "There," she said, and indicated a clock on the desk, facing the sofa on which she sat. It had showed, unbelievably, that the time was almost two o'clock.

It had taken her two hours of struggle to get one hand free, to wriggle from the sofa to the floor and, there, reach the cord of the telephone and pull the instrument to the floor beside her. How, with her hand only partly free, she had managed to dial Phoebe James's number —

"I don't know how I did it. I thought — I thought I would never get it finished."

"Why —" Pam began, but Nan Schaeffer spoke quickly.

"I knew Phoebe had a key," she said. "She's had it since — since Sam died, when she was coming here to — to help. To get things straightened out."

And now the two women looked at Pam North and, it seemed to her, there was a peculiar intensity in their regard. It was as if they were demanding something from her. But she did not know what they wanted. There was something which eluded her — her mind reached for it and it slipped away. It was as if they were demanding an answer from her, seeking to force her to some decision. Under the pressure, her uncertainty of its purpose, Pam felt herself growing uneasy. What did they want of her? What —

"It's strange the police don't come, isn't it?" Pam North said. "It's been quite a long time now and —"

She stood up, and moved toward the table by the heavy sofa — it was, she realized absently, a sofa which could be converted into a bed — and toward the telephone which one of them had put back on the table.

"I'm going to call them again," Pam said. "I know Bill Weigand's special —"

The others looked at her. There was, Pam thought, a puzzled expression in Nan Schaeffer's eyes — an expression, perhaps, of uncertainty.

"I know I —" Nan began. "It's all — it was all so confused before you came. Perhaps

252

they didn't — But they'd have traced the call."

Pam began to dial the seven stages of a New York City number. It would be hard, she thought — it must have been almost impossible — to dial while you lay on the floor, only one hand free — a thing essentially so easy must under those circumstances have been agonizingly difficult. W — A — 9 —

But then she heard the sound; they all heard the sound. In the big living room, someone was moving. The sound of steps was sharp as someone crossed a bare area of the oaken floor.

Pam stood, her hand motionless above the telephone dial.

"They've come back," Phoebe James said, in a whisper. "Hear them? *They've come back!*"

Pam looked at Nan Schaeffer. Nan's expression was still that of a person deeply puzzled. But now it was more than that. Nan listened to the steps in the room outside, and listened with an expression of entire incredulity.

They had been delayed, first by the telephone call which had come through as they were leaving the office in the West Twentieth Street station, then by Weigand's own decision as he drove, slowly through snow deepening on the pavement, up Park Avenue.

The telephone call had been from Detective

Thackery, who had a report. Early in the morning — probably about three or four o'clock — burglars had forced their way into the offices, in West Forty-second Street, of Sneed & Mallet, Private Investigators. "It's a crummy little outfit," Thackery had said. "Even as they go, crummy. Oughtn't to have a license. Mallet was in the car when they put the blast on Halpern. Remember?"

"Right," Bill said.

"Still in the hospital," Thackery said, and did not try to keep pleasure out of his voice. "Got it right where he had it coming — in the tail."

"Yes," Bill said. "Where you'd expect. So?"

The safe in the Sneed & Mallet offices had been broken open, according to Oscar Sneed's "squeal" to the precinct. Sneed professed not to know what had been sought, since no money was kept in the safe. "Not very much to keep anywhere, probably," Thackery said. Sneed had hinted at confidential documents of great value. "Who some guy went to a hotel with," Thackery interpreted. Sneed had also said that some tape recordings were missing and then, rather hurriedly, not very convincingly, had said that he dictated reports on a tape recorder and had them transcribed. This, considering the grubby modesty of the Sneed & Mallet operation, the investigating detective had considered improbable. The office equipment appeared to consist of two typewriters, three desks and a filing cabinet — which also had been ransacked.

"So," Thackery said, "looks like it might tie in, doesn't it? A tape on the wire tap. Maybe there was only the one, maybe some others. Anybody'd take them all along, of course. Went to the lawyer's office first and didn't find what they were looking for — didn't even find the transcription, because Karn had taken it home with him. Had a shot at Sneed's place, and apparently got what they wanted. Or — maybe they did. There's no way of telling. Sneed's not going to tell. Guy can lose his license for a private tap."

"Yes," Bill said. "It could tie in."

"We might take it up with Mallet," Thackery said. "He's in good enough shape. Just has to lie on his belly. Could be that would make him talkative."

It might, Bill agreed, be worth trying. Would Thackery see it tried? Thackery would.

Weigand and Mullins had left, then, and driven through Twentieth Street to Fourth Avenue, and up it, around Grand Central, into Park. But, when they were a few blocks above the Waldorf, Weigand had swerved the Buick into the curb and said they might see if the doctor had got back yet.

Dr. Aaron Arn had got back. He was, however, examining a patient. And, had they an appointment?

They had not; on the other hand, what they wanted would take only a minute or two. If Dr. Arn was not going to be too long?

They waited. They waited half an hour, and Bill Weigand seemed quite content to read the September issue of the *Atlantic Monthly*. This surprised Sergeant Mullins, because usually at this stage — or what he had taken to be this stage — the Loot was trying to be in half a dozen places at once, or to reach one place in no time flat. From the way he acted now, you'd think they had a month. It occurred to Sergeant Mullins that perhaps the Loot felt they had, which indicated they were not at the stage he had thought. Mullins sighed, and continued to look at the July issue of *Esquire*. *Esquire* wasn't what it had been. Full of reading matter, nowadays.

"And remember, no sauces," Dr. Arn said, from behind a well-filled-out man of sixty, who had an expression of mingled relief and perturbation on a plump face, who said, "Well —" in a tone of doubt. "For six months anyway," Dr. Arn said. "Then we'll see. Hello. You two again?"

He took them into the inner office.

"There," he said, "goes a man who will pay no attention whatever to what I tell him. He'll have four drinks and dinner at Chambord."

"And?" Bill said.

"Stomach ache," Dr. Arn said. "What can I do for you?"

"You have trouble with patients not doing what you tell them?" Bill Weigand asked.

"What doctor doesn't?" Arn said. "You didn't come here to ask me that?"

"As a matter of fact," Bill said, "I did. In a way. About one patient — man named Schaeffer. He didn't follow your instructions, did he?"

Dr. Arn looked at Weigand for some seconds, and looked through shrewd eyes.

"Apparently he didn't," Arn said, finally.

"You'd have expected him to?"

"I never expect much," Arn said. "If they do half what I tell them —" He smiled, faintly. "I won't say I don't make allowance for that," he said.

"Specifically," Bill said, "about Schaeffer. What did you expect from him?"

"Good sense," Arn said. "I never bet on it. But — he seemed a sensible man. A man who, when he knew where he stood, would adjust himself to it. Apparently he wasn't."

"Perhaps," Bill said, and stood up. "Perhaps he didn't really know where he stood, doctor. Thanks."

"That's all?"

"For now," Bill said.

He went, and Mullins went after him. In the car, they pulled out from the curb, skidding momentarily. At the next even-numbered street they turned east. The windshield wipers swished against the snow; the heater and defroster motors hummed steadily. Weigand let the traffic set his pace.

The footfalls came nearer; the man — the sound was surely of a man's heavier shoes — seemed to be coming toward the door under the staircase in the living room. But then the sounds altered, became those of a man climbing stairs. Heels clicked, twice, against the metalled bindings of the stair treads. Pam North looked at Nan, and Nan's head went back with the sound as if, through the wall, she could see the intruder mounting.

Pam looked at Phoebe James, and found Phoebe looking at her. The gaze seemed measuring, as if Phoebe were making up — or seeking to make up — her mind about something of importance. Yet Pam was not sure that she was, except incidentally, the object of this considering gaze. It was possible, she thought, that Phoebe saw nothing outside her own mind.

"Who?" Pam said, in a whisper, and Phoebe shook her head slowly. "Perhaps we could —" Pam said, and looked at the door.

"No," Phoebe said. "They'd hear us. We would get half across the room. We —"

"A back way?" Pam asked, still in a whisper, and Phoebe looked at Nan. But Nan did not seem to hear. She sat with her head back, still looking upward — although the sound of the man's climbing had ceased.

"Into the garden," Phoebe said. "Then through the garage. But —"

She did not finish; she only listened. The man was coming back down the staircase against the living room wall. He reached the foot of the stairs.

Then the man spoke. He spoke Nan's name; spoke it loudly in the big, echoing room beyond the doors. I've heard that voice, Pam thought, and at the same instant, Phoebe James said, excitedly, "It's Reg, Nan. Don't you hear — it's just Reg."

There was relief in her voice and, only on hearing it, did Pam realize they had sat, each alone, but still in a community of fear.

"Just Reg," Phoebe repeated.

Nan looked at the door, now. She looked, and waited, and her slender shoulders rose, as with a deep breath.

"Yes," she said, slowly. "I hear it is."

But it was Phoebe James who, after waiting a moment, called out — called, *"Reg. We're in here. In the library."*

There was the sound of a door opening then, and of quick steps.

XI

Reginald Webb was tall in the doorway of the little library, looking at three women, at first without speaking. He was tall and immaculate; the thinnest edge of a white handkerchief meticulously marked the breast pocket of a gray suit; the well considered knot of a gray and maroon tie nestled between the spreading, not overly-long, collar points of a white shirt. (If only Jerry would go to so much trouble, Pam thought, the irrelevant flickering across her mind.) Only Reginald Webb's face was in disorder.

He looked from one to the other, and looked, seemingly, in bitter anger. His brows were drawn together; there was a deep line between them. His mouth was a hard line across his face. His gaze ended on Nan Schaeffer, and held there.

"What the hell have you been doing to yourself?" he demanded of her, and his voice was harsh.

261

"I?" she said. "To myself, Reg?"

"What are you doing here?" he said, as if he had not heard her answer. "Don't you know —" But then he broke off. "You're hurt," he said, and now in a different voice. "How'd you get hurt?"

"One of them hit me," she said. "With the barrel of a revolver. I —" She put her hand up to the bruise. "After they brought me here last night," she said.

"They?"

"Two men," she said. "The ones — they must have been the ones who stopped you. Threatened you. They were looking for something. I walked in on them. The man with the tight mouth."

"All right," he said. "All right. Let's get out of here. This is —" He broke off again. "Get a doctor to look at you," he said. "Have you called the police?"

"I —" she said, and looked at Phoebe James, at Pam North. "I called them. I don't — I guess they didn't get it right."

"She called me, Reg," Phoebe James said. "We — Mrs. North was there. We found her tied up."

He looked at Phoebe James, then, and his eyes narrowed. It seemed to Pam that, unspoken, some thought — some understanding — passed between them. But she thought, from Webb's face, that it was the understanding of enmity.

"Tied up?" he said.

"Yes," Phoebe said. "But she got a hand loose to dial the telephone. I untied the rest. Mrs. North got a knife but —"

"All right," Webb said again. "We'll have to get you out of here, Nan. It's no good your being here." He took a step toward her. But she drew back.

"I'm all right," she said. "All right now."

"They found Mary's body," he said. "They're looking for a man — or a boy. A kid in a loose coat. Or — they say they are."

"Mary?" Phoebe James said. "Mary Burton?"

He nodded, very briefly.

"Mary too," Phoebe said. "But — why Mary?" She looked at Webb, shifted her gaze to Nan. "Why Mary?" she repeated, and it seemed to Pam that this was unexpected to her, and surprising — as finding Nan tied on the floor, as hearing Webb calling from the big room, had not been.

"I don't know," Nan said. "How could I? I was here. They wouldn't let me go." She paused. *"Wait!"* she said. "The man driving their car — the boy, really. And — they said something about a ferry? Did I tell you that?"

She asked of Phoebe, of Pam North.

263

"You told us that," Phoebe James said. "You remember she did, Mrs. North? Mrs. Burton lived on Staten Island, you know."

Pam was not sure she had known; she was not sure of anything — except that the three of them were somehow together, and she alone; except that, in the momentary silence, sleety snow beat against the tall, curtained window of the small room.

"She said something about a ferry," Pam said. "I remember that. But —"

"When was she killed?" Nan asked, and spoke hurriedly.

"Yes," Webb said. "That's important, isn't it? Sometime this morning — an hour or so after midnight."

"That's where he went, then," Nan said. "The boy who was driving the car. But — why? As Phoebe says — why?"

Webb merely looked at her. He shook his head slowly.

"She must have known something, mustn't she?" Phoebe James said. "Wouldn't you think that, Mrs. North? Something about — about Forbes's death?"

(She keeps drawing me into it, Pam thought. As if — as if to be sure I'm listening? To get me to — to what? To commit myself to something?)

Pam nodded. She reached for the telephone.

"No," Webb said. The word rasped. "We don't want the police yet, Mrs. North. We're not ready yet. Are we?" He looked at Nan. "Are we?" he repeated.

"I don't know what you mean," she said. "What do you mean, Reg?"

"Oh —" he said. "We want to get you to a doctor. Have him look you over — see if you're all right. Before you have to — go over all this with the police. Tell them about the men who tied you up." He turned to Pam. "That's reasonable, isn't it?" he said. "It's better that way."

Again Pam North felt that she was, for some purpose she did not understand, being drawn in as — but as what? Then she thought, I'm supposed to remember this — all of this.

"She seems all right," Pam said. "It's — it's just a bad bump and —"

But she stopped at a sudden thought: *Why, it is really just a bad bump!* The kind you get if you walk into a door in the dark. The kind you put cold water on, and get a headache from and —

"No," Webb said. "She needs a doctor."

"Of course," Phoebe said. "More than a bump, Mrs. North. She was knocked out. Don't you remember? She was unconscious for — for a long time."

She looked at Pam intently.

"Whatever it looks like," she said. "Whatever it looks like to you."

Webb moved impatiently, again toward Nan Schaeffer. "Come on," he said. "Get a coat. You've got a coat here?"

"I —" she said, and looked around the room. "I must —"

"It's in the closet across the hall," Pam North said. "I saw it when I was looking for the knife. It's hanging up in the closet." She paused. "On a hanger," she said. "They — they must have hung it up for you, Mrs. Schaeffer. Instead of just —"

"All right," Webb said. "I'll get it."

He turned quickly, was through the door. Now it was Nan Schaeffer who looked at Pam with an odd intensity.

"Why do you make —" she began, and then stopped as Webb came back into the room, carrying the mink coat, holding it out toward her. She stood and looked at the coat, and then slowly began to shake her head.

"Come on," he said, and spoke roughly. "We haven't got forever."

She shook her head again.

"One of them said, 'Where'd you put it? After he gave it to you?' " she said. "I just remember that. Did they mean you, Reg? That you had given me something? The list they talked about?"

266

He lowered the coat. It touched the floor. He noticed this, or seemed to. He lifted it so that it was free of the carpet.

"I don't know what 'they' meant," he said, and he emphasized, faintly, the word "they." "I didn't give you anything."

"No," Nan said. "But they thought you had. They must have meant you. Why would they think that, Reg? What would —"

"You didn't tell us this before," Phoebe said. "Did she, Mrs. North? Only now."

"I just remembered it. I said that."

"Yes," Webb said. "They heard you say that, Nan. You'd better come — better let me take you to a doctor."

"To a doctor?" she said. "Is that it? Are you sure that's it, Reg?" She drew back. "No," she said. "I — I think I'd rather wait. I don't need a doctor. I'm — *you weren't mixed up with them, were you, Reg?* In something Forbes found out about and —" She stopped. She drew back still farther. "I guess not," she said. "I guess not."

He looked at her. Then he looked at Phoebe James, and then at Pam, and his gaze seemed to measure all of them.

"No," he said, "You don't need a doctor, Nan. You're doing fine." He faced her, seemed to seek to force her to meet his gaze. But she did not. "Yes," he said. "You're doing fine, Nan. I might have known you would."

"Well," Phoebe James said, "were you mixed up with them, Reg? These people Nan talks about? The ones she says were looking for a list? Some kind of a list?"

"You're doing fine too," Webb told her.

"I'm going to find out who killed Forbes," she said. "Don't you want to find out? Or — *don't you need to, Reg?*"

"And Mary Burton," Nan Schaeffer said, and spoke quickly. "Did you send —"

Webb laughed suddenly. His laughter was as harsh as his voice had been. Pam felt he was laughing at himself. His laughter died as suddenly as it had begun, and then they heard someone knocking on the distant street door, the sound echoing in the big living room on which the door opened. For a moment no one spoke, and in the silence the distant knocking seemed very close.

"Your friends are back, Nan," Webb said. "Very noisy friends."

And then all three of them looked at Nan Schaeffer, and saw her eyes narrowed, her whole expression one of extreme concentration. She was — she was, Pam thought, like a cat, eyes narrowed in speculation, wondering from which direction danger threatens, wondering in which direction it is safe to leap.

"No," Phoebe said. "Not her friends. Because — they've got your key, haven't they, Nan? It must be the police — the police finally. It —"

The knocking was more peremptory.

"Well," Phoebe said, "are we waiting for them to go away? Is that what we're waiting for?"

Still, for an instant, no one moved. Then Pam North moved; moved around Reginald Webb, who did not try to stop her; moved along the short corridor to the living room and, in it, moved more quickly still, until near the door she was almost running. She pulled at the heavy door, got it open, and snow came blowing in and Pam said, "Oh. It took you long enough," to Bill Weigand and Sergeant Mullins.

"You turn up in the damnedest places," Bill said, and came into the room with Mullins behind him, and they brushed snow from overcoats. Bill stopped brushing and looked beyond Pam and said, without emphasis, "So this is where you all got to." Pam turned. Nan and Phoebe had come into the room and stood under the stairs, and Webb stood, looking very tall in shadows, behind them. They came further into the room.

Nan Schaeffer broke from the others and almost ran across the room. She clutched the mink coat in her arms, and did not seem conscious that she held it.

"Thank God," she said. "*Oh, thank God! I thought nobody would ever come.*"

"Now lady," Sergeant Mullins said, "just take it easy. You're all right now."

"They brought me here," she said. "Right from the hotel. All night and today and they tied me up and —"

"By they," Webb said, and he too — he and Phoebe James — came further into the room. "By they she means two men, one with a small, tight mouth. The men I told you about, captain. She thinks — she says, anyway — that I'm mixed up with them." He paused momentarily. "I told her about them at dinner last night."

"Did you?" Bill Weigand said. "Right, Mr. Webb. That's quite a bruise you've got there, Mrs. Schaeffer. One of the men hit you?"

"With a revolver," Nan said. "He —"

But she stopped, because Bill Weigand did not appear to be listening. Instead, he was looking around the big room with tall windows on two sides, with the iron staircase angling up a third wall. It occurred to Pam, preposterously, that Bill might have been inspecting with a view to purchase. What he said seemed to bear out this preposterous supposition.

"The bedrooms," Bill Weigand said. "They're up there, Mrs. Schaeffer?"

270

"What?" she said. "The — what did you say?"

"The bedrooms," Bill said again. "Open off the balcony. That's right, isn't it?"

"Why," she said. "Yes. But —"

"A long climb up," Bill said. "And — a long way down."

"You —" Nan Schaeffer said. "Why do you say that? Bring it all — bring it all back?"

"Mrs. Schaeffer's husband fell on the stairs," Bill said, and now he spoke to Pam North. "Fell all the way down. Stumbled at the top and fell. He'd started down to — what did you say he'd started down to do, Mrs. Schaeffer?"

"I didn't know," she said, and was staring at Bill Weigand. "How could I have known? Sometimes he went down to get something to eat — a glass of milk. When he couldn't sleep."

"Yes," Bill said. "I remember now. That was in the report. These men, Mrs. Schaeffer. Why did they bring you here?"

"They were looking for something," she said. "A — a list of some sort."

"And you thought Mr. Webb was — what did you say? — mixed up with them?"

"I — I didn't know," she said. "They were all so strange — Reg, Phoebe, Mrs. North, even. And —" She laid the coat on a chair.

"I'm not myself. I'm — I feel all mixed up." She touched the bruise on her temple. "It hurts again," she said. "I don't know what I said."

But Pamela North did not believe her and then, with a sudden kind of completeness, realized that that was what had been wrong — been wrong for a long time. She had not believed any of it — not the two men, not the blow on the temple, not the —

"Bill!" Pam said. "Listen. She —"

"In a minute, Pam," Bill said. "In just a minute."

"No," Pam said. "Please listen. It's just the kind you put cold water on, really. And, a call from a dial telephone can't really be traced in — oh, for a long time. But everybody doesn't know that. And the coat — look at the coat, Bill!"

And then, as if her words compelled them, they all looked at the mink coat, very glossy, very beautiful, on a chair — laid, most carefully, in a most orderly fashion, over the back of the chair. It seemed to anticipate a caress.

Pam was expectant. She looked at Bill.

"But," she said, "it's all very clear. As clear as anything."

"I don't know what she's talking about," Nan Schaeffer said. She looked around at the others.

"Don't you, my dear?" Phoebe James said. She spoke softly, and yet she spoke with hatred. "Don't you? Oh — I think you do, Nan." She moved a step closer to Bill Weigand. "That was why?" she said, and she pointed at the staircase.

"Yes," Bill said. "That was why. Where was your husband really sleeping, Mrs. Schaeffer?"

"What are you talking about?" she said. "I don't — my head hurts. You wanted to take me to a doctor, Reg. Take me — take me now."

She swayed, and put out a hand to the back of the chair nearest her.

"No," Reginald Webb said, and seemed to speak from a great distance. "It's no good now, Nan." He paused. "You want it too many ways," he said. "That's the trouble with you, Nan."

"Please," Bill Weigand said. "One at a time. You say they kept you here last night, Mrs. Schaeffer? And today? Until — until when, would you say?"

"Until — oh, the middle of the afternoon," she said. "What are you talking about? About Sam? About —" She shook her head, and held both hands to it. "I'm all mixed up. You keep — you keep jumping around so."

"Yes," Phoebe James said. "Oh yes. You're mixed up."

"One of the men had a small mouth — a tight mouth, you say? And the other was taller, and did most of the talking?"

"Yes," she said. "I told you that. Anyway —"

"The man with a tight mouth is named Horse," Weigand said. "They call him that. He took a midnight plane to Chicago. The other man probably was a man named Smithson. He went to Miami on an eight o'clock plane. This morning."

"It couldn't —" she said. "I'm not sure about the man's mouth. I —"

"No," Bill said. "I guess you're not, Mrs. Schaeffer. And —"

"Bill," Pam said. "You won't listen. The coat hung up in the closet. So carefully. They wouldn't have and the way she told it she didn't have time. And not calling the police last night, but Jerry and me instead, because she thought the call could be traced and she probably was on her way to Staten Island. And today, although it's easy to dial O instead of all those numbers, the police would have known the knots weren't right and —" She paused. "Bill," she said. "Why didn't you look here?"

"Oh," Bill said, "the precinct boys came here, of course. Got here about one this morning. The place was closed up tight, no lights

274

on. They couldn't raise anybody. As Mr. Webb can tell you, we don't break in. Don't break the law."

"All right," Webb said. "I tried to get her away. Because —" He stopped. "The hell with it," he said.

"It wasn't that," Nan said. "Oh — it wasn't that. He was afraid I'd — afraid of what I'd say. Because — all this about Sam — that isn't it at all. Reg was mixed up in —" Then she stopped and looked around at all of them. And suddenly, because of what she saw in their faces, she dropped into a chair and covered her own face with her hands.

"The point was," Bill Weigand said slowly, "that her husband was under doctor's orders not to over-exert himself. Not to run for subway trains, as he wrote Ingraham. And not to climb stairs, of course. He must have slept —"

"In the library," Pam North said. "There's a sofa there that turns into a bed."

"Probably," Bill said. "How did you get him to climb the stairs, Mrs. Schaeffer? Call down that you'd hurt yourself, needed help? And then — just how did you do it, Mrs. Schaeffer?"

Nan Schaeffer did not answer, but only pressed her prettily manicured hands more tightly against her face. Reginald Webb looked at her for a moment and then walked to one of the tall windows and stood looking out at the snow. But Phoebe James did not take her eyes off Nan Schaeffer, and there was hatred in her eyes.

XII

They had been playing tennis and were of pinkish hue — a hue which Pam North called "preliminary pink." Jerry was also somewhat damp. Nevertheless, since it was a time of day at which dampness was to be expected, they stopped at the desk for mail. The mail was generally of an uninspiring sort, and included Monday's New York *Times*, mysteriously forwarded. It included also a long envelope from the Police Department, City of New York, the initials "W.W." appearing above the printed return address.

They carried mail to their room, which was not large, but had a very large window — a window level with the tops of coconut palms, a window from which the sea was visible. The window was open and warm air came gently in.

"I promised to fill in whatever gaps remain," Bill Weigand wrote them. "The simplest way seems to be to send you this carbon. I don't need to say that it's confidential, hasn't been published and probably won't be until the trial. They'll fight admission then, as usual; probably fail as usual. Meanwhile — destroy after reading or, at any rate, conceal. Right?

"She didn't hold out as long as I expected.

"Now — unless there's a hitch, as no doubt there will be — Dorian and I will fly down at the end of next week and may be able to spend three or four days. It's snowing again here.

"Until then, with all envy,

"Bill"

"P.S. Incidentally, we've got the goons who broke into the office to thank for turning up Schaeffer's letter, which, of course, put us on the track."

"They're coming," Pam said, and handed the letter to Jerry, who had reduced his costume to shorts and was lying on one of the beds. "If nobody important gets killed west of Fifth Avenue." She held up the several sheets to which the letter had been attached. "Shall I read and pass?" she said. "Or do you want to be a pig?"

"Read and pass," Jerry told her. "I'll lie and pant."

"It doesn't begin at the beginning," Pam said, after she had looked. "And it's Q and A."

"All right," Jerry said. "You read it and then I'll read it. O.K."

"Um-m-m," Pam said. "It was an assistant D.A. A Mr. Phillips. Do we know Mr. Phillips?"

"Please, Pam," Jerry said. "I don't think so. If you're going to read it aloud?"

Pam shook her head. She said, "For heaven's sake!" She said, "Imagine doing that." Jerry waited. Pam finished the sheet and held it out. Jerry read:

Q. (By Mr. Phillips) He hadn't been sleeping upstairs for some weeks, then?

A. No. On the sofa downstairs.

Q. His heart was affected?

A. I guess so. He always babied himself. Pretended he didn't want sympathy but —

Q. Yes. You told us that. But you did believe he hadn't told anyone else of this?

A. That's what he said. And then he wrote this letter to Forbes and . . .

Q. And you got him to come up that night by saying that something was wrong with the toilet? That it was overflowing and you couldn't stop it? And met him at the head of the stairs and caught him off balance and pushed him down?

A. All right. But you make it sound . . .

Q. Mr. Ingraham showed you this letter? Said that it made him doubt — would make

279

anyone doubt — that your husband had been climbing up and down those stairs. In view of —

A. He threatened me. He threatened to —

Q. Please let me finish, Mrs. Schaeffer. In view of the doctor's advice, and the fact that Mr. Schaeffer was the kind of man to take that advice — as Mr. Ingraham knew. Expecting his clients to take his advice as a lawyer, Mr. Schaeffer made a point of —

A. You go over it and over it. Forbes threatened me. Said he would go to the district attorney and have the whole thing dragged up again. What could I do?

Q. This was on Monday? When Mr. Ingraham said he was going to the district attorney?

A. I told you that. On Monday.

Q. And the next day you used the key — the gold key — you hadn't returned with the rest of your husband's keys, and went through your husband's office and into Mr. Ingraham's. And shot him?

A. I told him I hadn't killed Sam. I asked him please not to bring it up again.

Q. And when he said he was going to, you shot him? With a revolver you had brought with you, in your purse?

A. He threatened me.

Q. You shot him?

A. I — I tried to frighten him.

Q. You shot him? Killed him?

A. Yes.

Q. Before that, he had asked you for the key? You had got it out of your purse and put it on the desk in front of him? And it was while he was picking the key up and putting it in the top drawer of his desk that you shot him? While his attention was distracted?

A. Yes. I suppose so — yes. . . .

Q. Mrs. Burton called you up Tuesday evening? Said she remembered the key hadn't been with the others?

A. She never got things straight and —

Q. But she had got that straight, hadn't she? You hadn't returned the key. Why hadn't you, Mrs. Schaeffer? You didn't, then, know you were going to use it to get to Mr. Ingraham? So you could kill him?

A. Of course not.

Q. Then — why?

A. I — it was a gold key. A special key. I'd had it made and paid for it myself and —

Q. Go on, Mrs. Schaeffer.

A. That's all. It was mine. When a thing's yours you — take care of it.

Q. The way you did your coat — hanging it up in the closet in the apartment? And the things in your hotel suite — when you were trying to make it appear that the rooms had been searched?

A. (No verbal answer. The witness nodded her head.)

Q. You tried to persuade Mrs. Burton you had really returned the key? But you weren't sure you had and decided that she — how did you put it? — threatened you? As Mr. Ingraham had?

A. Yes, I suppose so.

Q. You don't deny that you went to Staten Island in your car? Wearing slacks and an old hat of your husband's? And a loose coat — a top coat? You don't deny that you got Mrs. Burton to let you in, or that you shot her?

A. All right. Can't you leave me alone now?

Q. Very soon, Mrs. Schaeffer. You admit you killed Mrs. Burton?

A. Yes. Yes. She was a muddle-headed old fool and I couldn't be sure that . . .

Q. You got the idea of this kidnapping pretense after Mr. Webb told you of the men who stopped him? Figuring it would provide you with an alibi for the killing of Mrs. Burton? And, of course, since her death and Mr. Ingraham's obviously were linked, eliminate you from that, too? In case you were, eventually, suspected?

A. Forbes threatened me, I tell you. What could I do? He . . .

Q. The reason you called the Norths from — it was from a booth at the ferry house, wasn't it?

A. Yes. I told you that.

Q. Was because you thought a call to the police could be traced?

A. Yes. Yes. Yes. Yes.

Q. There are only a few more questions, Mrs. Schaeffer. Wednesday afternoon — when you decided it was safe to be found — you called Mrs. James, and not the police. You didn't call the police at all, did you?

A. No.

Q. Called Mrs. James because you thought the police wouldn't be fooled by the way you were tied up? Would know that it was something you had done yourself? Tried to do. Whereas Mrs. James would untie you — or cut the cords — without noticing anything?

A. You're very clever. You're all very clever. That North woman! That little . . .

Q. And hit your head against the iron railing of the stairway? That must have been hard to do, Mrs. Schaeffer.

A. You can do things you have to do . . .

Q. Why did you kill your husband, Mrs. Schaeffer?

A. (No answer)

Q. Come, Mrs. Schaeffer. You've been co-operative up to now. By the way — we haven't offered you any inducement to tell the truth, have we? You've made this statement of your own free will? Without being promised special consideration?

A. God. Oh *God! Of my own free will!*

Q. Well, wasn't it? Were you promised anything? Forced in any way?

A. You've been at me for hours. Over and over and over.

Q. Did we promise anything? Use any form of compulsion?

A. You have to have that, don't you? All right. You didn't promise anything. Of my own free will, I, Nan Schaeffer, do . . .

Q. (By Acting Captain William Weigand) Why did you kill your husband? For the insurance money?

A. (No answer)

Q. Because Mr. Webb wouldn't have an affair with his friend's wife? With the wife of a man who was his partner, whom he respected, who had —

A. Conceited, yellow, priggish little . . .

Q. It was because of Mr. Webb, then?

A. You think he was the only man around? The only man . . .

Q. Why did you kill your husband, Mrs. Schaeffer? If not for money, not because of Mr. Webb —

A. Did you ever see him? Any of you? The

old flabby fat man — the — you want to know why I killed him — he made me sick to look at him and when —

(The witness became hysterical at this point and it was necessary to give her a sedative. A formal statement embodying the foregoing, was prepared and signed the following day.)

At the foot of the last page, Bill Weigand had written: "The Halpern angle, as you see, had nothing to do with it — just one of those things that crop up to make a policeman's life an unhappy one. Webb does tell me he's keeping Halpern on as a client. Quite a man to do the right thing, Mr. Webb is."

Jerry North put down the last sheet and whistled softly. "Of all the reasons," he said.

From Pam who was stretched on the other bed, he received no immediate response. He turned to look at her, and found that he was himself being regarded — with, Jerry thought, rather special attention.

"Oh," Pam said. "You've finished?"

"Yes," Jerry said. "Why were you looking —?"

"Who showers first?" Pam said. "Shall I go ahead and —?"

She stood up and began to remove her tennis dress.

"It's almost lunch time," Pam said. "If

we're going to get a drink before lunch, and it's the buffet in the patio and that always takes a long time. Such a big lunch."

Jerry regarded his slender wife, ready now for her shower. He watched her as she went into the bathroom, heard the water begin to run. Jerry North reached for the telephone by the bed. He got the tennis professional on the telephone. He arranged for an hour's practice at three. It would be a good, stiff workout. Well, his backhand could certainly stand it.

Gerald North leaned back against the pillow and lighted a cigarette. Absently, he patted the abdomen which, he could not doubt, had been the object of Pam's particular regard. Poor Schaeffer, Jerry thought — probably hadn't had a lick of exercise in years. Enough to make any man lose balance at the top of a flight of stairs.

THORNDIKE PRESS hopes you have enjoyed this Large Print book. All our Large Print titles are designed for easy reading, and all our books are made to last. Other Thorndike Large Print books are available at your library, through selected bookstores, or directly from the publisher. For more information about current and upcoming titles, please call or mail your name and address to:

THORNDIKE PRESS
PO Box 159
Thorndike, Maine 04986
800/223-6121
207/948-2962